Mail Order Marvel

Book 27 in Brides of Beckham

Kirsten Osbourne

Chapter One

Elaina Walstad stood looking around her father's ranch, her green eyes reflecting the vast Montana sky. She adjusted the brim of her hat against the glare of the afternoon sun, her strawberry blonde hair fluttering untamed in the prairie wind. The expanse of rolling fields and distant mountains had been her childhood playground; now, they were her responsibility, her legacy.

"Jasper, I asked for those fences to be mended by noon," Elaina called out. The cowboy she addressed paused, wiping sweat from his brow with a dirt-streaked forearm before responding.

"George said we should move the herd first, Miss Walstad," Jasper replied, avoiding her gaze. "He said it'd be better for grazing."

A muscle twitched in Elaina's jaw. Her father's passing had left a void in leadership that George—an older man who had been on the ranch since before she was born—seemed intent on filling. But it was her land now, her decisions to make.

"George isn't running this ranch," Elaina stated, more to herself than to Jasper. The cowboys had worked under her father's command for years, and their loyalty to George was unshakeable. They were not easily swayed by the authority of a woman, even if she was their employer.

"Tell George I want to speak with him," she ordered, her tone leaving no room for argument. Jasper nodded silently and set off toward the barn.

Elaina surveyed her land, the weight of her inheritance pressing down upon her. She knew the ropes as well as any man—her father had seen to that—but respect was not given freely in this world, it had to be earned or taken. The cowboys saw her as a figurehead, a relic of her father's time, but she would show them the steel beneath her skin.

Elaina squared her shoulders, ready to reclaim her birthright one command at a time. George would listen, or he would leave. This was her land, her life, her father's legacy, and she would fight for it with every breath in her body.

Elaina's boots crunched the brittle, frost-kissed grass as she made her way to the barn. The air was sharp with the scent of pine and impending winter, a chill that seeped through her heavy woolen coat and into her bones. As she neared the structure, voices carried on the wind—George's gravelly tones laced with authority that wasn't his to wield.

"Boys, make sure the cattle are rotated to the south pasture come morning," George commanded, his voice echoing off the wooden walls of the barn.

Elaina halted behind the half-closed barn door, peering through a gap just wide enough to afford her a view of the cowboys gathered around George. Their heads bobbed in agreement with every word he uttered.

"Shouldn't Miss Walstad be deciding that?" It was a young hand. Elaina recognized him by the pitch of his voice.

"Miss Walstad has enough on her plate, don't you worry," George replied. "She needs us to take charge of these decisions. Besides, I know this land better than anyone."

Elaina felt the sting of suspicion twist in her gut like a knife. She'd seen it before, the subtle undermining, the sly looks exchanged when they thought she wasn't watching. George had been her father's right hand, but now his ambition was clear. He wanted control, and he was planting seeds of doubt among her men to get it.

"Jasper!" Elaina called out, stepping into the barn with a forcefulness that caused a hush to fall over the group. "Get those cattle ready for the north pasture. That's where they're headed tomorrow."

A murmur of surprise rippled through the cowboys, but Jasper nodded, casting a wary glance between Elaina and George.

"North pasture, ma'am," he confirmed, and Elaina could almost taste the sweet victory of her command being followed.

"Good night, George," she said, her gaze fixed firmly on the old cowboy.

With her chest tight and her mind racing, Elaina retreated to the sanctuary of her home. The fire crackled in the hearth, casting a warm glow over the spartan furnishings of the living room. She sank into her father's old chair, the leather creaking under her weight as she contemplated her next move.

It was clear she needed someone by her side. Not just any man, but one who was willing to stand with her, who could manage the ranch and its stubborn hands. Someone who could help her shoulder the burden and respect her authority. A partner in every sense of the word.

The idea of a mail-order groom, once a fleeting thought, now took root in her mind. It was unorthodox, perhaps even scandalous, but Elaina was past caring for the whispers of society. She needed a man of substance. Someone who would see the value in her determination and match it with his own.

Determination hardened within her like the frozen ground outside. Tomorrow she would pen a letter to a matchmaker back East she'd heard people talk about, entrusting her to find a man up to the task. A man who could help her reclaim what was rightfully hers and restore balance to her world.

Elaina allowed herself a moment to dream of a future filled with hope and companionship. One where her voice was heard and her commands were followed out of respect and shared vision.

ELAINA SAT AT HER FATHER'S old desk. With a pen in her hand, she wrote to the matchmaker she'd heard such good things about.

Dearest Elizabeth Tandy,

Your reputation as a matchmaker of unparalleled skill has traversed the miles, finding its way to me, filling me with hope during these trying times.

My name is Elaina Walstad, and I find myself penning this letter under the heavy mantle of both duty and desperation. The land I call home, a sprawling ranch nestled in Montana, has been my sanctuary and my challenge. Yet, I face trials that weigh heavily upon my spirit.

The root of my problem lies with my foreman, a man whose intentions have grown increasingly suspect, casting shadows of doubt over my lands. I fear he is planning to find a way to take my ranch from me.

The situation at the ranch has become untenable. Since my father's passing, the cowboys have grown unruly, refusing to acknowledge my command. They are loyal to George. However, I fear his intentions are not as honorable as they once seemed.

George's influence over the men is considerable, and I suspect he seeks to undermine my position for reasons I cannot yet discern. It has become clear that I require a partner—a man of character and fortitude—to stand beside me.

Thus, I turn to you, Mrs. Tandy, with a request that carries with it the weight of my hopes and dreams. I seek a companion, a partner, not just in marriage, but in the stewardship of this land.

I yearn for a man who is used to hard work, be it through farming or ranching. His character must be strong and his spirit kind.

This man would find here not just a position of trust and respect, but a home filled with warmth. Together, we would run my ranch the way it should be run.

I place my trust in your hands, believing in your ability to find the one who would complete this picture, and who would bring balance to my life. In return, I offer my sincerest gratitude and the promise of a partnership forged in honesty and respect.

With warmest regards and in hopeful anticipation,

Elaina Walstad

Her request was unorthodox, yet necessary. Elaina needed more than just a hired hand; she needed a man who could shoulder responsibilities and share in the vision she held for her land.

Sealing the letter with wax, Elaina imprinted it with the Walstad family emblem—a lone tree standing resilient against the elements. As she turned the letter over in her hands, her mind's eye cast forth images of a stalwart figure riding up to her homestead, a man whose eyes would meet hers with understanding and whose presence would bridge the divide between her and those who doubted her leadership.

Elaina considered having one of the ranch hands take her letter into town to mail, but she thought better of it, deciding she should take it herself. She had no idea whether or not George had told the men that all correspondence must go through him.

She allowed herself to dream but only for a moment. To imagine a man who would stand by her, who would listen and be a partner in every sense.

"Enough daydreaming, Elaina," she murmured to herself as she turned toward the stable to saddle her gelding, her boots kicking up the earth in decisive steps. "There's work to be done."

"Father, I will not let our legacy crumble," she whispered to the empty room. Her breath made the flame of the oil lamp flicker, casting dancing shadows over the walls, like spirits of the past urging her forward.

STEVEN MILLER FINISHED mucking out the stalls in the barn before heading to the farmhouse where he'd grown up. He needed lunch and a short break from his labors. It was spring, and there were new calves to look after. He and his father were planting their crops for the year.

As the youngest son in the family, and the only one left at home, it was his responsibility to help his father with all the chores around the farm. Only he and Ida Mae, the youngest of his sisters, were left at home. He missed the years when the work was lighter because of the many hands that were there to help get everything done, but he was happy to have more space to move around in the house.

Just as he reached the house, he spotted a buggy, and his sister Elizabeth was in the driver's seat. It was strange to see her without her husband, Bernard, but it was always so good to see her. Though they lived a short distance from one another, they went to different churches, and Elizabeth was part of a different social group than the rest of the family.

He raised his hand in a wave to Elizabeth and walked to where she had stopped the buggy. "You never visit during the week!" he said. "What are you doing out here?"

Elizabeth smiled. "I came to see you."

He frowned. "You only ever come to see your brothers if you want them to marry."

She sighed. "I wish I had more time to spend with all of you, but you're right. I'm here because I have a woman who I think would be ideal for you."

Steven shook his head. "I don't want to be one of your mail-order grooms, Lizzie. It just doesn't seem like something I would enjoy."

"Let's discuss this," Elizabeth said. "What is your dream for your life?"

Steven thought about the question for a moment. "Moving west and starting a ranch." It had been in the back of his mind as a dream for years, but he'd never dared speak it out loud.

Elizabeth reached into her jacket pocket and pulled out a letter, handing it to him. "Just read it."

He frowned at the letter. "I don't want to marry a stranger."

"Please, Steven. You need to trust me."

He sighed, unfolding the letter and reading through it. When he was finished, he looked at his sister, and he understood. "She needs not only a husband, but a manager for her ranch. Someone who will take orders from her but will also be able to give orders to the men."

"Yes," Elizabeth said simply.

"Montana? That's a long way."

"It is. But I think it's the perfect situation for you, don't you?"

Steven stared at his sister. "I do. How did you know that was my dream?"

She smiled. "All of my brothers have had the same dream. And we both know, no woman around Beckham would marry a former member of the demon horde."

He chuckled. "Being part of the demon horde is one of the most interesting things I've ever done."

Elizabeth shook her head. "But now you have to rise above it, and you can't do that here."

"You're right," he said softly. "Maybe I should do this."

"Ma and Pa won't mind," Elizabeth said softly. Most of their siblings were already married off and had been matched by Elizabeth.

"I want to think on it for a day or two. I'll come into town on Friday evening, and we'll talk. Does that work?"

Elizabeth nodded. "Though, I think you need to decide quickly or there won't be much of a ranch left to go to."

As Elizabeth drove away, Steven thought about how much he'd love to have his own place. A ranch where he could call the shots. Along with his wife, of course. It would be like he was a hero of old, riding in on a white steed and fixing all her troubles. And she'd be so grateful to him for his part in getting her out of hot water.

It seemed like the perfect life for a man like him. A man who needed to get away from his past and marry, starting a legacy of his own. And he'd have an easy time starting that legacy with Elaina waiting for him and helping him to run the ranch that was her inheritance.

The more he thought about it, the more he realized it was exactly what he wanted and needed from life. That evening he rode into town and talked to his sister, who suggested he leave immediately.

She gave him the address of the ranch, and he took it, looking at it almost reverently. He was going to live a life full of love. And he was going to do it while working for himself and building a cattle ranch into the biggest and most profitable place west of the Mississippi.

He left two days later, getting on a train that would get him to Montana and his future. His father could handle the work without him. It had been nice to have two sets of hands working toward family goals, but he knew his father didn't truly need him. Not like Elaina did.

As he watched the world pass by his window on the train, he thought about how wonderful it was going to be to meet a woman who would immediately marry him, who knew nothing about the demon horde. Maybe people around Beckham looked down their noses at him and his entire family, but in Montana, no one would understand what he'd done to earn his reputation.

He was going to be a respectable rancher, and that was all there was to it. And he'd have a beautiful bride who would cook for him and keep the house clean while he dealt with the men. His life was going to be exactly what he needed it to be.

Chapter Two

Steven Miller reined in his newly purchased horse, the expanse of Elaina's ranch sprawling before him. The wild grandeur of the West lay open and inviting, with skies so vast they promised freedom and renewal. Yet, as Steven's gaze descended upon the ranch itself, a sobering sight replaced the spark of hope that had carried him this far.

Dilapidated buildings dotted the property. The barn, its red paint faded to a mere whisper, sagged under the weight of neglect, its doors hanging off hinges too tired to protest. The corral lay in disrepair, its broken fence posts jutting out.

As he urged his mount forward, Steven's eyes swept across the fields, where weeds had claimed the land meant for grazing. The soil was parched and cracked, and he wanted to plow it all up and plant something. He noted the stunted growth of the garden.

A sense of duty stirred within him. The land was aching for revival, and Steven felt the weight of responsibility settle upon his broad shoulders. He knew the labor would be backbreaking, but the land called to him.

The horse beneath him snorted, uneasy with the stillness that hung over the place, and Steven offered a calming pat to its neck, whispering assurances to both the animal and himself. "We've got our work cut out for us, boy," he murmured.

He dismounted with the grace of a man accustomed to the saddle. In the distance, the mountains stood watching over everything. He wished they could tell him of the things that had happened since Elaina's father had died.

Steven set his jaw with quiet determination. With each step toward the heart of the ranch, Steven embraced the challenge that awaited him, ready to breathe life into this corner of the West that time had seemingly forgotten.

Steven was examining the splintered wood of the corral fence when he heard the sound of approaching footsteps. He straightened, turning to see a woman walking toward him. She moved with purpose, her long strawberry-blonde hair trailing behind her.

"Mr. Miller?" Her voice carried across the expanse, a clear note in the vast silence of the ranch. As she drew closer, Steven could see the resolve etched on Elaina's face, her green eyes lit with intensity.

"Miss Walstad," he greeted, tipping his hat in respect. "I've just arrived."

Elaina stopped before him, her gaze taking him in. "I hope your journey was tolerable. There's much to discuss and even more to be done," she said. The weariness of her tone made him wonder how long she'd been fighting against her father's men to do the job.

"I agree," Steven replied. "You mentioned urgent matters in your letters. I'm here to assist in any way I can."

She sighed. "It's the foreman," she began, hesitating for a fleeting moment before the floodgates opened. "He's been betraying my trust, selling off my cattle under pretenses. The profits were substantial, and none made it into the ranch's ledgers."

Shock rippled through Steven's frame, a silent wave that tensed his shoulders. His hazel eyes narrowed sharply. "Selling your cattle?" he asked, disbelief lacing his words. "How long has this been going on?"

"Months," Elaina admitted. "Since shortly after my father passed. I only found out recently. The foreman was careful, but not careful enough."

"Miss Walstad," Steven said. "I give you my word, we'll set this right."

Elaina's eyes searched his. She gave a curt nod, the flicker of gratitude apparent despite her efforts to remain composed. "Thank you, Mr. Miller. Your promise gives me hope."

"I think we need to figure out exactly what he's been doing," Steven suggested.

"Agreed," Elaina said. "It's not going to be easy, and I know the foreman won't give up when he's challenged. But we must protect what's rightfully mine."

Steven looked up at the sky, seeing that the sun was starting to set. "Are we going to marry today? Or do you want to wait a day or two before we get the legalities out of the way?"

Elaina didn't like her wedding being referred to as legalities, but she knew that he was right. She didn't need rumors flying around about her character at such a difficult time for the ranch. "Let's ride into town and get it done now." She started toward the stable, aware that he was right behind her.

When they reached the stable, Steven saddled a horse for her. "You sure you don't want to take a buggy?" he asked.

"I'm sure. I don't know what women are like where you're from, but I can tell you that around here, women can take care of themselves."

Steven shook his head. "My sisters are perfectly able to spend the morning cooking, the afternoon helping birth a cow, and the evening planting crops. I assure you, I will not underestimate you because I know full well what women can do."

Elaina nodded. "Good, then you won't argue with me when there's work to be done."

"Do you cook?" he asked.

"No, my mother died when I was a girl and never taught me. We have a live-in cook who has been around for as long as I can remember."

He nodded. "Just so someone is feeding us," he said with a grin.

They made the ride into town without saying much else to one another. It was hard to carry on a conversation with both of them riding into town. Once there, she led the way to the church, and then behind the church building to the parsonage. The pastor made the wedding quick, and soon they were on their way back. As they rode back, he realized the pastor hadn't invited him to kiss her, which had been what he'd wanted out of the ceremony. It didn't matter though. He'd find a way to kiss the girl before the night was over. She was too beautiful not to.

When they got back, they wiped down their horses and put them in stalls for the night. "I want to show you one more thing before we go eat our supper," Elaina said, needing him to understand what they were up against.

"Over there," Elaina said, pointing to a dilapidated fence line, "the foreman promised it'd be mended come spring. It seems he was more interested in lining his pockets than upholding his word."

Steven followed her gaze, noting the sagging posts and the barbed wire hanging limp. He reached out, letting the coarse strands run through his fingers before they fell away. "We'll need to take inventory of what supplies we have—if any. And gather able hands willing to work for honest pay."

"Most of the men are loyal to him," Elaina's voice broke slightly. "It won't be easy to convince them otherwise."

"Then we will start small," he assured her, "with those who value integrity over deceit. The truth has a way of rallying folks to a just cause." Steven shook his head. "Tomorrow, I'll begin by talking to the hands, gauge where their loyalties lie."

They continued on, stepping around a broken wheel that lay abandoned near the barn, its wood splintered and gray. The structure itself leaned precariously, its doors hanging askew.

"Here," Elaina said, stepping into the house and handing him a ledger she'd kept. "I've tried keeping track, but without knowing how much cattle he's sold..." She trailed off, a look of frustration etched across her features.

"Let's sit down tonight and go through this together," Steven suggested, taking the book from her. "We'll compare it against the brand registry, and see if the numbers match up. Any discrepancies could help us expose him."

"I'm glad one of us is confident we can work this out," Elaina admitted. "I can't thank you enough for coming all this way."

"Miss Walstad...I mean, Elaina," he replied solemnly, "helping you restore this place to its rightful standing isn't just a duty—it's an honor. This land," he gestured broadly out the window, "it deserves to be nurtured by someone who truly cares. And I intend to ensure that happens."

Elaina's lips curved in a tentative smile, the first genuine expression of hope Steven had seen since his arrival.

"Tomorrow," she said, "we begin anew."

Looking out, Steven noticed a figure standing atop a small rise that overlooked the ranch. The foreman, his arms folded across his chest, watched the house. His stance was casual, but there was an unmistakable tension in the way he held his shoulders.

Steven felt Elaina tense beside him as her gaze followed his to the solitary man. The foreman's weathered face seemed carved from the same tough leather as his boots, and his eyes, though distant, carried a flicker of something akin to guilt—or perhaps fear.

"He knows something is up," Steven said softly.

"His name's George," she said quietly, "and he knows his days here are numbered."

After supper, Steven sat with her ledger and worked on the numbers by lantern light. Elaina watched him work. "I've never seen anyone so thorough," she remarked.

"It's what I do," he replied without looking up. "Or at least, it's what I did for my family's farm back in Massachusetts. My father always said, 'A man's worth is measured by the integrity of his work.'"

"Your father sounds like a good man."

"He is," Steven answered simply.

Hours passed as he combed through the records, cross-referencing receipts and tallies, his keen eye catching several entries that didn't add up. He circled them one by one, the ink from his pen stark against the yellowed paper.

"Here." He tapped a line item dated several months prior. "This sale—it's marked as fifteen head of cattle, but the brand count for that week decreased by twenty. That's money unaccounted for, money that should be in your pocket, not his."

Elaina leaned closer, squinting at the details. "How could I have missed this?"

"Because you trusted him to be honest," Steven said. "And he took advantage of that trust."

They locked eyes, and in that moment, an unspoken vow passed between them. They would right these wrongs, together.

"Tomorrow," Steven declared, "we confront George. We'll demand answers, and if he can't provide them, we'll take our evidence to the sheriff."

"Thank you, Steven," Elaina said. "For everything."

He shook his head, dismissing her thanks. "No need for that. We're in this as partners now, aren't we?"

"Partners," she repeated. "Come with me. I'll show you the room that will be yours for now. I think you'll understand that I don't want to share a bed with a man I just met a few hours ago."

Steven nodded. "I do understand that, but I want one kiss before we say goodnight."

She frowned at him. "My pa would never approve."

"Probably not. But he's not here to argue with us, is he?" He turned to her fully outside the door to the room that he would be using. "May I kiss you, Elaina?"

Elaina nodded. "I suppose I owe you at least that much after all the work you've already done for me."

"No, you owe me nothing. I'm asking for a kiss. Not from a grateful woman who wants my help with her ranch. I want a kiss from Elaina given freely to her new husband."

Her eyes widened, and she licked her lips without thinking. "All right."

He caught her waist in his hands and leaned down, pressing his lips to hers. It was a light kiss...one with the entire purpose of learning her taste, and letting her get used to his touch. When he lifted his head, he saw that her eyes were closed and her lips were parted slightly. "Goodnight, Elaina."

"Goodnight, Steven."

STEVEN ROSE WITH THE sun. He dressed quickly ready to start his day. As he stepped out onto the weathered porch, he caught a glimpse of Cynthia bustling around the kitchen, the golden morning light spilling through the open door.

"Good morning," she called out. "I'll have breakfast ready soon."

"Thank you, Cynthia," Steven replied. The woman was older, perhaps not old enough to be his mother, but she was at least thirty-five.

"Elaina mentioned you might need some help getting acquainted," Cynthia said as she wiped her hands on her apron and joined him on the porch. "The men can be a tough bunch to crack. Loyal to a fault, especially to George. You're going to have your work cut out for you."

Steven gazed across the expanse of the neglected property, feeling the weight of the task ahead. "Any advice on how to win them over?" he asked.

"Be fair, but firm," she advised, leaning against the porch railing. "They respect strength, but more than that, they need to see that you care about this land just as much as they do. And," she added, "they've been working under a man who's been lining his own pockets at the expense of the ranch. They might not know it yet, but they need someone like you."

"Someone like me?" Steven asked. For all she knew, he could be worse than George.

"Someone who sees beyond the horizon," she said. "These men, they've seen bosses come and go, promises made and broken. Show them you're different."

He nodded, absorbing her words. "I'll do my best."

"Elaina believes in you," Cynthia said, pushing off from the railing. "And I've got a good feeling too. Now, come get some breakfast. You'll need your strength."

This was more than just a job—it was an opportunity to restore something that had once been grand. With each cowboy he could convince to see the truth, they would rebuild not only the fences and the finances but also the heart of the ranch itself.

"Let's start after breakfast," he said, meeting Elaina's steady green gaze across the table. "One step at a time."

"Exactly," she replied. "We'll do this together."

After breakfast, Elaina and Steven set out across the ranch, spotting two men working. With a leather-bound ledger under his arm, he approached the corral where the men were mending a break in the fence.

"Morning," Steven called out.

Beau looked up first, his sandy hair sticking to his forehead, a skeptical twist to his mouth. "Morning," he replied.

Elaina looked between the men and her new husband. "Steven, this is Beau and Nathaniel. They've worked for the ranch for years. Men, this is my new husband, Steven. He's the boss around here now."

Nathaniel grunted, his eyes flicking toward Steven with an appraising squint before returning to his work. "Steven," he acknowledged.

"Got a moment?" Steven asked, leaning against the fence post. He held out the ledger for them to see. "I'm implementing a new system for tracking the cattle—tags for each one, numbers corresponding to this book here. We'll know exactly what we have at all times."

The cowboys exchanged a glance, the weight of their loyalty to the old ways—and to the foreman—etched into the lines of their faces.

"Seems like a lot of extra work for something we've been doing just fine without," Beau said.

"Maybe," Steven conceded, "but we haven't been doing just fine, have we? The foreman's been lining his pockets while the ranch suffers."

Nathaniel stopped hammering and straightened, his stocky frame casting a long shadow. "You got proof of that?"

"Working on it," Steven admitted. "But I need you two to trust me. Help me set things right."

The silence stretched out, taut as the barbed wire they were stringing. It was Nathaniel who broke it, his voice a low rumble. "What do you need us to do?"

"First, help me get these tags on the cattle. Then, we start keeping track of every sale, every expense. Tighten up the financials so not even a penny goes missing without notice."

"All right." Beau nodded slowly. "I reckon if it's for the good of the ranch, we can give it a try."

"Good," Steven said, relief threading through his resolve. "Let's get started."

As they worked side by side under the relentless sun, the rhythmic sounds of their labor punctuating the quiet, Steven felt the tentative beginnings of camaraderie. Beau, with his easy grin that seemed to reappear as he warmed to the task, and Nathaniel, whose silent nod spoke volumes of his emerging respect.

With each tag secured and each entry marked in the ledger, Steven's vision for the ranch became clearer—not just a place to live and work, but a home, a community bound by shared purpose.

By day's end, the new system was in place, and Steven watched as Beau and Nathaniel stepped back to survey their handiwork. Their initial skepticism had given way to cautious optimism, reflecting in their weary smiles a hope that maybe, just maybe, things were changing for the better.

"Looks good," Nathaniel said, clapping Steven on the back with a rough hand. "Never thought I'd say it, but...this might work."

"Thanks, Nathaniel," Steven replied.

"Suppose we'll see soon enough," Beau added.

"We sure will," Steven agreed. They would face resistance, no doubt, but today's progress was a testament to what they could achieve.

Much later, Steven noticed George leaning against the corral. The old cowboy's gaze was like a sharpened blade, cutting through the darkness and settling on Steven with a weight that spoke of unspoken challenges.

"Evening, George," Steven called out.

"Miller." George's reply was gruff. "Been hearing about these changes of yours. Not sure I like what I'm hearing."

Steven approached slowly, boots crunching on the gravel. He knew that gaining George's trust would be no easy feat. But to get the other men to trust him, George had to trust him first.

"Change can be good, George. We're just trying to do right by the ranch," Steven offered.

"Maybe so," George muttered. "But some folks don't take kindly to outsiders stirring the pot."

The underlying threat in George's words hung in the air, a reminder that loyalty could be both a blessing and a curse. Steven nodded. As he walked away, the sound of whispered conversations and furtive glances followed him like shadows.

Back inside the main house, Elaina was hunched over a ledger, her hair cascading around her shoulders like a fiery curtain. Her green eyes lifted as Steven entered, a spark of resolve igniting within them.

"Any luck with George?" she asked, her voice a mix of hope and concern.

"Hard to say," Steven admitted, sitting opposite her. "He's set in his ways. But I believe he'll come around once he sees the ranch thriving again."

Elaina closed the ledger, her fingers tracing its worn edges. "We can't afford to lose any more time," she said firmly. "If we don't expose George soon, there might not be a ranch left to save."

Steven nodded, sharing her sense of urgency. "Tomorrow, I'll start digging into the records. If the foreman's been as sloppy with his deceit as he has with the ranch, we'll find something."

"Be careful, Steven," Elaina cautioned, her brows knitting together.

Steven reached across the table, covering her hand with his own. "I didn't come all this way to back down now," he assured her. "We're in this together, Elaina. And we're going to bring him to justice, one way or another."

WITH A DEEP BREATH, Steven turned his gaze to the neglected fields, their potential choked by weeds and disrepair. Each broken fence post, each untended acre was a symbol of the foreman's betrayal.

The ranch house door creaked open, and Elaina stepped out onto the porch, her silhouette framed against the dim interior. She was already dressed for the day's labor.

"Morning," Steven called out, his voice steady despite the uncertainty that lay ahead.

"Good morning," Elaina replied. "Did you sleep?"

"Enough," he said, though his mind had wrestled with strategies and contingencies well into the night. The foreman's deceit was a tangled web they would have to unravel.

They walked side by side toward the barn. Steven knew that each cowboy under the foreman's influence could be a spy, every shadow a hiding place for treachery.

"Beau and Nathaniel will be here soon," Elaina mentioned, her tone carrying a hint of gratitude for the two allies they had found among her staff. "They agree with your plan to implement the new tracking system."

"Good." Steven felt a glimmer of hope at that. If they could secure the loyalty of a few, perhaps others would follow.

"George won't make this easy," Elaina cautioned, her gaze lingering on the bunkhouse where George reigned supreme. "He has the others' ears."

"Then we'll speak louder with our actions," Steven resolved. "We'll show them what this ranch can be, what they've lost under his leadership."

Chapter Three

Early the following morning, Steven strode into the dusty paddock where the cowboys were beginning to gather. He could feel their eyes on him. There was tension in the air, and he knew they were all worried about whether or not they would keep their jobs.

"Morning, gentlemen," Steven greeted, his voice steady and clear. The cowboys muttered responses, their tones ranging from grudging respect to open hostility.

"George," Steven nodded toward the older cowboy who leaned against the fence, arms folded across his chest, his steely blue eyes sharp beneath the brim of his weathered hat.

"Steven," George acknowledged with a curt nod. "You planning on changing things around here?"

"Changes that need to be made to improve the ranch," Steven replied, meeting George's challenge without flinching. He knew he couldn't declare war on George outright, though it was difficult not to.

A younger cowboy spat tobacco juice into the dirt, his sneer evident. "And you think you're the man to do it? Just because you married the boss doesn't mean you can march in here and play lord of the land."

Steven's hazel eyes swept over the group, his posture unyielding. "I'm not here to play at anything. This land, these cattle, they're all part of our livelihoods. I aim to see that we're doing the best we can for them—and ourselves. Anyone who doesn't want to follow me is welcome to leave."

"Sounds like a lot of pretty words," George countered, pushing off from the fence to stand squarely in front of Steven. "But words don't move cattle or mend fences."

"True enough," Steven conceded. "Which is why I plan to show you through action. You'll see the fruits of what I propose soon enough. And you'll also see that I'll be there with you every step of the way, working as hard—if not harder—than every other man here."

"Or we'll see this place run into the ground by some greenhorn from back East," one of the cowboys muttered, earning a few chuckles from his companions.

"Perhaps," Steven said, undeterred. "But I've worked land before. Different soil, same principles. And I've got ideas—ones that could make this ranch thrive if you're willing to give them a chance."

"Like what?" George demanded, eyeing Steven skeptically.

"Rotating the grazing areas more frequently, for one," Steven explained. "Improves the health of the grass and the cattle. And diversifying our livestock— maybe introducing some sheep. It's risky, but it could pay off."

"Risky? That's putting it lightly," George scoffed. "Cattle and sheep don't mix. You'd start a range war with a fool notion like that."

"Only if we handle it poorly," Steven maintained. "We can set up separate grazing areas. It's been done successfully elsewhere." Steven had spent time reading about agriculture for years. Some men read novels or poetry. He read about building empires.

"And if it fails here?" George pressed.

"Then we adapt and try something else," Steven answered simply. "Because doing nothing isn't an option. Not if we want to survive and see this place grow." He shook his head. "Looking around this ranch, I can see many things were let slide. The buildings are in disrepair. Some of the land has been used to pasture the cattle too often. Some barely at all. We're going to correct those mistakes, and make this ranch the best in the entire state of Montana."

The cowboys exchanged wary glances, the seeds of doubt sown among the lines of resistance. George held Steven's gaze for a long moment before finally stepping back.

"Time will tell, I suppose," George said gruffly.

"Indeed, it will," Steven agreed. "We're rotating the grazing fields effective immediately. I've marked out the new boundaries on these maps." His finger traced the lines he'd drawn the night before.

"New boundaries?" one of the cowboys, a wiry man named Hank, questioned with a furrowed brow.

"Correct," Steven responded, meeting Hank's gaze squarely. "It'll ensure we don't overgraze any one area. Keeps the land healthy, the cattle fed."

Murmurs rippled through the group, but Steven continued undaunted. "I've also scheduled repairs for the north fence line starting tomorrow—"

"Repairs? The foreman never bothered with that rickety old thing," another cowboy interjected.

"Which is exactly why we're fixing it," Steven replied smoothly. "Can't have the cattle wandering off or worse, getting injured."

There was a pause as the cowboys digested his words, their expressions a mixture of skepticism and curiosity. Steven took advantage of the silence, handing out the maps and instructions with a quiet confidence that seemed to steady the lingering doubts.

"George, I want you leading the team on that fence. You know the terrain better than anyone."

George received the map with a nod, a grudging respect beginning to dawn in his eyes.

"All right, boss," he said, and the single word held the weight of a turning tide.

"Thank you, George," Steven said.

As Steven continued to delegate tasks, Elaina emerged from the ranch house. She approached quietly, standing just within earshot.

"Steven," she spoke softly during a lull. "The boys are talking. They're seeing the sense in your plans. Your strength is giving them something to lean on."

He glanced at her and felt a warmth that wasn't from the sun. "I appreciate your faith, Elaina. It means more than you know."

"Faith is easy when you see things changing for the better," she replied. "Look at them, they're listening now. And they're ready to follow."

Steven watched as the men began to disband, their steps more purposeful than reluctant. There was still much to do, many challenges lying in wait, but the spark of hope that had been so elusive under the foreman's rule had been struck anew.

"Let's get to work," he said. With the ledger tucked under his arm once more, Steven turned back to the tasks at hand.

STEVEN STOOD WITH A hammer in his hand, watching the fence line where the cowboys worked—or rather, where they were supposed to be working. The posts lay scattered, and the men's efforts were lackluster at best. George leaned against a rail, his thumb hooked in his belt loop, defiance etched into the lines of his weathered face.

"Mr. Miller," George drawled, "We've been fixing fences the same way for years. Your 'new method' just doesn't sit right."

Steven considered the man with patience worn smooth by countless such confrontations. "I understand your concern, George," he said calmly, "but we need to try different methods if we're going to improve the ranch. The old ways haven't been keeping the cattle in. Too many have gone missing."

"Seems like a waste of good daylight," one of the younger cowboys muttered, kicking at the dirt.

"Perhaps," Steven conceded with a nod. "But a few hours spent learning now could save us days of chasing strays later on."

The cowboys exchanged hesitant looks, but after a moment, they shuffled back to work. Steven didn't miss the shared glances, the subtle rolling of eyes. He walked over, picked up a post, and began to demonstrate the technique once more, his movements precise and assured.

"Like this," he instructed, positioning the post. "It'll hold better against the winds and the weight of the cattle."

The new method proved more challenging than Steven had anticipated. Posts refused to stay put, wires snapped, and tempers frayed. Yet, Steven's demeanor never wavered. When a particularly stubborn post caused frustration to flare, he simply took a step back, wiped the sweat from his brow, and approached the problem from a different angle—literally and figuratively. He dug a little deeper, angled the post slightly to the left, and when it finally held firm, there was a collective nod of approval from the cowboys.

"Seems you might be onto something, Miller," George admitted as the day came to a close.

"Thank you, George," Steven replied, clapping the older cowboy on the back. "We're all here to make this place better. Tomorrow, it'll go smoother. You'll see."

That evening, Steven found himself sitting beside Elaina on the porch of their home. Her hand found his, fingers intertwining.

"Today was hard-fought," Elaina said softly, her gaze on the horizon. She'd spent some of the day helping with the fences.

"But worthwhile," Steven added, giving her hand a gentle squeeze. "They're starting to come around."

"Your patience is something to behold, Steven," she said warmly. "You lead with a quiet strength that draws people in."

STEVEN STOOD ATOP A small rise, surveying the land that stretched out before him. He felt it then, a quiet thrumming in his veins—a confidence born not of pride but of the tangible results he could see in the neat rows of repaired fences and the cattle grazing contentedly in the lush fields.

"Looks like the herd's taken to the north pasture quite well," Elaina remarked, joining him on the hill with a basket of fresh laundry hooked on her arm.

Steven turned to her, the corners of his eyes crinkling in appreciation. "That they have, thanks to your idea to rotate the grazing areas. It's made all the difference." He watched as she shook out a shirt, snapping it in the air before folding it neatly. "You've got an eye for the land. Your insights have been invaluable. You obviously learned a lot from your father."

She blushed at the compliment, ducking her head slightly. "I'm just glad I could help."

"More than help," Steven insisted. "You've been a cornerstone in all of this." His gaze swept across the ranch—their ranch—and he knew that without Elaina's support, none of it would have been possible.

Later that afternoon, Steven found Elaina in the stables, expertly brushing down one of the mustangs. He leaned against the stall door, watching her work with an ease that spoke of years spent tending to these powerful animals.

"Got word from the blacksmith," Steven said, breaking the comfortable silence. "He'll be out next week to shoe the horses."

Elaina nodded, her strawberry blonde hair catching the sunlight filtering through the slats above. "Good. I was thinking we should expand the south paddock. Give the mares more room."

"Agreed," he replied. They talked on, mapping out plans for irrigation and crop rotation, their conversation was a seamless exchange of ideas and shared visions.

After supper that night, he turned to her. "Thank you, Elaina," he murmured earnestly. "For believing in me. For standing by my side."

She smiled, a soft, genuine curve of her lips that reached her eyes. "We make a good team, don't we?"

"We do," he agreed, his heart full.

"LOOKS LIKE THE NEW irrigation ditch is holding up," Elaina observed, walking up beside Steven. The soil beneath their boots was moist, a testament to Steven's foresight and strategic planning.

"Looks like it," he replied, nodding. "If we're lucky, it'll carry us through the dry spell and keep the pastures green."

"George came around today," Elaina said, her voice tinged with relief. "Said you're doing things differently, but maybe not all bad."

Steven's lips quirked in a half-smile. "I'll take that as a compliment, coming from George.

"Tomorrow, we'll start training the new colts," Steven stated. "It'll be good for morale, and better yet for the ranch's future."

Elaina nodded, her silhouette framed by the fading light. "We'll need strong horses and stronger men if we're going to expand the cattle drives like you plan.

"Speaking of challenges," she continued, her eyes fixed on a distant point, "the Johnsons are putting up fences along the east ridge."

"Encroaching on our grazing land again?" Steven's voice was steady, but his mind raced with the implications. Disputes over territory were common, but with the ranch finally gaining ground, any setback felt monumental.

"Seems like it," Elaina confirmed. "We'll need to address it, sooner rather than later."

"First thing in the morning," he agreed, his resolve hardening. "We can't afford to lose an inch."

"Come on," Elaina said, touching his arm lightly, "let's head back. We've got plans to make and a future to build."

"Today was a victory," Steven murmured, his voice a low rumble in the quiet. His arm rested gently around Elaina's shoulders, drawing her close. She leaned against him, her body warm and comforting at his side.

"It was," Elaina agreed, her head tilting up to meet his gaze. In the dim light, her green eyes glowed with a mixture of pride and determination.

Their lips met. The kiss lingered, unhurried. When they parted, there was a new resolve etched into their expressions.

"Tomorrow, we'll ride out at first light to deal with those fences," Steven said, his thumb brushing softly against Elaina's hand. "I've been thinking about a way to approach the Johnsons—firm, but fair."

Elaina nodded, her mind already turning over the possibilities. "We'll make it clear that we're not to be trifled with. But we'll also extend an olive branch, maybe suggest a meeting between the families."

"Exactly," he replied. "And about the cattle—"

"Let's move them to the south pasture for now," she interjected, reading his thoughts. "It's less than ideal, but it'll buy us some time."

"Smart," he praised, his hazel eyes reflecting the last vestiges of daylight. He leaned in for another kiss, this one brief but full of the promise of partnership.

"Thank you," Steven whispered after a pause, his breath stirring the wavy tendrils of strawberry blonde hair at Elaina's temple. "For standing by me today. For believing in what we're building here."

She rested her head on his shoulder, wondering if he would soon try to make their marriage a real one. He'd been there for two weeks, and so many changes had taken place on the ranch. But they still slept in separate bedrooms. Was he not attracted to her?

Chapter Four

Elaina and Steven set out early the following morning and approached the modest homestead of the Johnsons, their nearest neighbors.

"Morning, Mr. and Mrs. Johnson," Steven called, his voice carrying easily in the still air. He tipped his hat respectfully.

"Good morning to you both," replied Mr. Johnson, a wiry man she'd known all her life. He'd been a few years ahead of her in school. His wife, a stout woman with dark hair, offered a warm smile that crinkled the corners of her kind eyes.

"Would you care to join us for supper on Saturday night?" Elaina's invitation was laced with a hopeful note. "We need to talk about the land, and I always think it's best to discuss important matters over a good meal."

"Delighted," Mrs. Johnson said. "We'll bring a pie—apple, if that suits."

"Apple'd be fine," Elaina assured, a genuine smile brightening her features.

As they turned and rode back toward their own home, Elaina smiled over at Steven. "I think that's going to go well. They're good people."

Steven nodded, his gaze traveling to where her button up blouse was tight over her breasts. He could imagine how she'd look if he slipped the buttons free and stripped it off her.

When she caught him looking at her, he looked away, not wanting to give his feelings away.

AS SATURDAY'S LIGHT waned into evening, the table was set with careful consideration, plates flanking a steaming roast, and cutlery gleaming under the flickering candlelight. The conversation flowed easily as the four of them sat together, discussing the weather and other unimportant things.

Steven carefully steered the conversation to the land. "We noticed you moved the fences onto our land again. I'd appreciate it if you would move them to the border between the ranches instead."

"See here," Mr. Johnson began, unfolding a worn map onto the table. "This here's the land left to me by my pa, borders marked clear as day."

Elaina retrieved her own map, laying it beside the Johnsons'. Her father's neat script labeled each parcel of land, but the boundaries didn't match. The lines diverged like forked paths, creating a silent tension that hovered over the table.

"Your map shows your land stretching a good quarter mile further west than mine," Steven observed, pointing to the discrepancy. His hazel eyes moved from the maps to their guests, seeking common ground rather than contention.

"And yours lays claim to the creek running through what we thought were our acres," added Mrs. Johnson, her brows knitting together in concern.

"Pa wouldn't have left me false information," Elaina said, her voice steady despite the uncertainty that flickered in her gaze. "But nor do I believe you'd be here with dishonest intentions."

"Nor would we," Mr. Johnson affirmed, his tone sincere. "Seems we're at an impasse, don't it?"

"I think so," Steven agreed, folding his hands on the table. "But there's sense to be made of this yet."

Elaina nodded. "Then let's find it."

Their eyes met, the unspoken agreement hanging in the air as tangible as the scent of apple pie that Mrs. Johnson had indeed brought, now cooling on the windowsill.

The Johnsons lingered by the stove, where the warmth from the dying embers offered a cozy reprieve from the night's chill. Steven leaned against the doorframe, watching the couple with an appraising eye.

"Perhaps we ought to visit the land office on Monday," he suggested, breaking the silence that had fallen over them like a comforting blanket. "Records there should set this straight."

"Sounds fair and square to us," Mr. Johnson said with a nod, his hands clasped behind his back. Mrs. Johnson gave an agreeable hum, her eyes reflecting the flicker of candlelight.

"Then it's agreed." Elaina wiped her hands on a cloth after putting the last dish away and turned toward them, her green eyes bright with resolve. "Whatever is officially recorded, we'll stand by it."

"Good neighbors make for peaceful hearts," Mrs. Johnson chimed in.

"Speaking of good neighbors," Steven interjected, "how about a game of cards to pass the evening?"

"Ah, now you're talking." Mr. Johnson's face lit up with boyish enthusiasm. "Euchre, Hearts, or poker?"

"Let's say Hearts," Elaina answered before Steven could speak, a playful challenge dancing across her features. She caught Steven's gaze and smiled, feeling as if they were truly a couple as they entertained their neighbors together.

The four of them gathered around the table, each taking a seat as Elaina produced a deck of cards, worn at the edges but no less inviting. They shuffled and dealt, laughter and conversation weaving through the air like threads in a tapestry, binding them closer with each turn of a card.

"Seems you've got quite the hand there, Mr. Miller," Mr. Johnson remarked, peering over his spectacles as Steven laid down a winning trick.

"Pure luck," Steven replied, though his hazel eyes sparkled with unspoken glee. Being raised in a family with more than a dozen children, he had always been competitive. At times like this, he was happy for the way he was raised.

"Or maybe it's the company," Elaina added softly. Her words, though quiet, carried weight, and the room fell into a comfortable lull, filled with the mutual recognition of newfound friendship.

"Reckon we're more alike than different," Mrs. Johnson mused, looking between Elaina and Steven. "All of us want nothing more than to live peacefully on this land we love."

"That's very true," Elaina agreed, her gaze lingering on Steven for a heartbeat longer than necessary.

As they played, Steven regaled them with stories about growing up in Massachusetts, telling them of the pranks he and his siblings played on everyone. "Everyone around called us the demon horde. We had so much fun. Ran off more than our share of teachers too."

The others laughed, and the spirit of camaraderie grew stronger, and when the hour grew late and the Johnsons took their leave, they all knew they'd be friends no matter what the land office said about the boundary between their ranches.

Left alone in the dimly lit room, Elaina and Steven exchanged a glance. In that quiet space, with the echoes of friendly laughter still hanging in the air, Elaina wished she knew how to let Steven know she was ready for their marriage to move onto the bedroom without coming right out and telling him, but she was at a loss.

Steven's gaze found Elaina, who stood by the hearth, her hands idly straightening the few items that had been displaced during their congenial gathering. The room seemed to hold its breath, the only sound the crackling of the fire and the occasional shift of logs turning to embers.

"Elaina," he began, "I really enjoyed this evening. I felt like we were a team with one purpose in mind."

She looked up, her eyes reflecting the flickering light, carrying within them an unspoken question. For a moment, everything else fell away.

"I agree," she replied, the corner of her mouth tilting upwards ever so slightly.

Steven took a step closer, his boots scuffing against the wooden floor, the sound grounding him. He felt the weight of his decision in his chest, a heaviness tempered by a burgeoning sense of rightness.

"Elaina," he said again, his hazel eyes steady on hers. "I think we've come to know each other well enough these past weeks. And tonight... tonight feels like a turning point." He paused, surveying her face for any sign of hesitation.

Her eyes never left his, and in their depths, he saw the flicker of understanding. "Steven, if you mean what I think you do..." Elaina's voice trailed off, but she stepped forward, closing the distance between them.

"I do," he confirmed, his heart hammering in his chest. "I'd like us to be a true husband and wife, in every sense."

Elaina's hand reached out, her fingers lightly brushing against his. "I would like that too," she whispered.

With a mutual agreement, they ascended the stairs, their movements deliberate and synchronized, as if the rhythm of their steps could pave the way for what was to come. The bedroom door swung open to reveal the modest space bathed in moonlight, casting shadows that danced upon the quilted bed.

Slowly, they faced one another, the air around them filled with anticipation and the promise of intimacy. Their hands met once more, this time clasping, as they each took turns shedding the layers of clothing that separated skin from skin.

Finally, they stood before each other, vulnerable and exposed.

Steven cupped Elaina's face with his large, calloused hands, gazing into her eyes with reverence. "You are beautiful," he murmured.

"Thank you," she breathed. "I've always felt like I was just a little bit too rough and tumble to be seen as pretty."

He smiled at that, his thumb tracing her lips. "Not by me. I'm as attracted to your strength as I am to the rest of you. You seem so strong, and yet, your body is so soft."

Together, they lay down, their bodies aligning with a natural ease. As they explored each other, their movements were unhurried, each caress a discovery, each kiss a revelation. He delighted in every inch of her body, as she was thrilled to receive his touch.

In the aftermath, they lay entwined, the silence comfortable, filled with a new closeness that transcended words. Outside, the world was vast and uncertain, but inside, they had found a sanctuary in each other's arms. Her last thoughts as she drifted off to sleep were of him and how glad she was they'd finally taken this step together.

AT CHURCH THE FOLLOWING morning, Elaina and Steven sat side by side, and bowed their heads in reverence as the preacher's resonant voice filled the air with words of hope and redemption. It was a sermon that spoke to the heart, weaving tales from scripture into the everyday struggles and triumphs of the congregation. Elaina felt a quiet sense of peace settle over her, a gentle reprieve from the challenges of ranch life. She hadn't felt peaceful since before her father had taken ill.

As the final hymn echoed through the rafters, Elaina clutched the hymnal close, her voice mingling with Steven's.

Exiting the church, Elaina shielded her eyes with a hand, the other still held by Steven. Their steps were unhurried as they lingered on the path, surrounded by the chatter of neighbors and the laughter of children playing nearby.

"Fine sermon today," commented Steven, his gaze warm upon Elaina.

"Yes," she replied. "It reminded me that there's always a fresh start, no matter what."

Before Steven could reply, a voice carried over to them, rough-edged and tinged with mockery. "Well, if it ain't the lady rancher. Walkin' like one of the boys, ain't ya, Elaina?" The speaker, a cowboy from their ranch, leaned against the fence, a toothpick rolling between his lips.

Heat flared in Elaina's cheeks, and her grip tightened on the hymnal. Her father had done his best to teach her to be a lady, but she'd been so busy learning to run the ranch that the lessons hadn't taken. She'd always felt like she was less than the other women around.

Steven's posture straightened, a protective glint in his hazel eyes. He stepped slightly in front of Elaina, his voice calm but edged with steel. "Elaina carries herself with more grace and strength than most men I know. And she's a better rancher for it."

The cowboy's smirk faltered under Steven's steady gaze, and he pushed off from the fence, muttering something under his breath before sauntering away.

"Thank you," Elaina said softly.

"Nothing but the truth," Steven replied, a smile tugging at his lips as he gently squeezed her hand.

As they walked away from the church, Elaina felt a surge of warmth for this man who stood by her without hesitation.

STEVEN AND ELAINA MOUNTED their horses, enjoying a ride together on their one day of rest. They rode side by side in companionable silence.

Elaina noticed it first—a disturbance in the pattern of hoof prints that crisscrossed the prairie. She pulled up her chestnut mare and pointed to the ground. "Look there," she said, her voice tinged with concern.

Steven dismounted and knelt, running his fingers over the tracks. They were fresh, diverging from the path the herd usually grazed along and leading toward the rocky outcrop at the edge of their land. His brow furrowed. "This isn't a stray cow," he muttered, scanning the terrain. "These were driven away...deliberately."

"George," Elaina's voice was low but laden with certainty. Her gaze met Steven's, and in that look, a silent agreement passed between them.

Without another word, they followed the trail until it disappeared at a creek, the waters likely washing away any further evidence. Anger simmered within Steven as they turned back toward the ranch, the fading light casting long shadows upon the ground. The tracks were fresh. This had happened since his arrival in Montana, and that made things so much more personal for him.

As they approached the stables, the other cowboys were finishing up the day's chores, the clanging of tools and low murmur of voices drifting on the breeze. George was among them, his bushy white beard unmistakable.

"George!" Steven called out, his voice carrying across the yard as he swung down from his horse. The cowboys paused, turning to watch as the newlyweds approached.

"Got something to explain, do you?" George's steely blue eyes narrowed, a defensive edge creeping into his tone.

"Tracks," Steven stated flatly. "Leading away from where the cattle should be, heading off our land. Someone's been rustling our stock, and we know that someone is you."

A hush fell over the men gathered around. George's face remained impassive, but his eyes flickered with something unreadable. Elaina remained on horseback. She watched George intently, her presence a silent show of unity with Steven.

"Prove it," George challenged, his stance wide, arms crossed over his chest.

"Enough cattle have gone missing to make a man wonder," Steven countered. "We trusted you, George."

The other cowboys exchanged glances. No one spoke, but in their silence was an acknowledgment—that the life they sought could not abide deception or betrayal.

Beau shifted uncomfortably, his sandy brown hair catching the last rays of light as he glanced at Nathaniel. The seasoned ranch hand's stocky frame seemed to brace against an unseen force, his hands clenching and unclenching at his sides.

"George," Beau started, breaking the silence that had fallen over them. "We saw you marking up those tallies—adding head that haven't been bought, and leaving off some that's been sold."

Nathaniel nodded, his graying hair nodding with him. "It doesn't sit right," he added, his voice low but clear. "We're all here trying to carve out an honest living. Can't be doing that with numbers twisted."

George's steely blue eyes flashed in the dimming light, his bushy white beard bristling as if it were part of his indignation. "Y'all got no proof," he spat. "I've run these books for years longer than any of you have saddled a horse."

But the other cowboys, once shadows against the failing day, formed a circle that seemed to close tighter around George. Their expressions were etched with disgust. They had ridden the rough trails together, faced the blistering sun and biting cold; their camaraderie was forged in the fires of shared hardship. George's deceit was a betrayal not just of numbers, but of the very bonds that held them.

"George," one of them muttered.

"Beau, Nathaniel—they speak true?" another asked, searching the faces of his fellow cowboys for confirmation.

"True as the North Star," Beau affirmed.

"Been counting the cattle myself," Nathaniel added, his quiet strength speaking louder than words.

There, under the emerging tapestry of stars, the truth lay bare. George, the grizzled old cowboy who had once commanded their respect, now stood isolated.

Steven's hand curled into a fist at his side, the muscles in his jaw clenching as he faced the man who'd been part of the ranch for as long as the Walstads had lived there. The moonlight cast a pale glow over George's features, etching deep lines of defiance and guilt on his weathered face.

"George," Steven said, his voice steady despite the tempest of emotions that raged within him. "I've heard enough. Your time here is done."

George's eyes flickered with something akin to surprise, quickly masked by a familiar obstinance. He squared his shoulders, his beard bristling like the mane of an old lion ousted from its pride.

"Yer makin' a mistake, boy," George growled, his voice low and guttural, but it lacked the authority it once held.

"Perhaps," Steven conceded, his tone unyielding as bedrock. "But I will not abide deceit on my land. You've broken trust with us all."

"Get your things," Elaina added, her presence beside Steven unwavering, her voice carrying the weight of finality. "You leave at first light."

George's lips parted, perhaps to protest or plead, but no words came. Instead, he nodded, his steel blue eyes reflecting the faint glimmer of defeat. He turned, his movements deliberate, and walked toward the bunkhouse where his belongings—a lifetime's worth—were stowed.

The other cowboys watched in silence, their expressions somber, the sense of betrayal lingering like the scent of rain on dry earth.

Steven felt Elaina's hand slip into his. Together, they watched the dark outline of George disappear behind the wooden door of the bunkhouse.

"Tomorrow will be different," Elaina murmured, her words tinged with both sorrow and hope.

"Better," Steven replied, feeling the truth of it settle in his bones. Tonight marked an end, but also a beginning. A chance for renewed faith and the promise of the better life they all sought.

Chapter Five

Elaina and Steven, with the Johnsons in tow, steered their horses down the dusty main street of town. Today, they would speak with the land officer about the boundary dispute between the two ranches. The land in question was important because there was a creek running through it, and there was never enough water.

"Hopefully, Mr. Pritchard will be able to clear this up without much fuss," Mr. Johnson remarked.

"From your lips to God's ears," Elaina replied, casting a hopeful glance at the Johnsons, who nodded in agreement, their faces etched with the same anticipation. She knew the other couple was as eager to settle this as she and Steven were.

Upon reaching the squat brick building that housed the land office, they dismounted, hitching their horses before stepping into the cool interior. The room smelled faintly of ink and old paper, a scent that brought an odd sense of comfort to Elaina. It reminded her that beyond these walls lay the permanence of written records.

"Good morning, folks," greeted Mr. Pritchard, looking up from a stack of ledgers with a practiced smile. "What brings you here on this fine day?"

"We're here about the property lines for the Walstad Ranch," Elaina said.

"Ah, yes. Let me fetch the official map." Mr. Pritchard disappeared into a back room, emerging moments later with a large, rolled parchment. He spread it across the desk, holding down the corners with a pair of brass weights.

Together, they huddled over the map. Lines intersected and diverged, creating a patchwork of ownership and boundary claims.

Elaina's finger traced along the edge where her ranch met the Johnsons' land, while Steven leaned in, his gaze intent and analytical.

"Here," Mr. Pritchard pointed with an aged finger, "you see, both your original claims were incorrect." His words hung between them as they absorbed the implications. On the map, a compromise presented itself—a sliver of neutral territory that could bridge the gap between their lands.

"Would this be agreeable to all parties?" he asked.

"It looks like the creek we're all so worried about is the border, so both ranches should have access," Steven said with a smile, looking at Mr. Johnson.

"I don't think we could have settled it better," Mr. Johnson said, nodding.

"Yes, I believe this will do just fine," Elaina said. "We can all live with this."

"More than live with it," Steven added, "we can thrive with it."

"Then it's settled!" Mr. Pritchard exclaimed.

Mr. and Mrs. Johnson looked pleased as they stepped back outside. "What a perfect solution," Mrs. Johnson said. "Perhaps you'll both come to supper on Saturday night, and we'll celebrate the ease with which this matter was settled. We could play hearts again,"

Elaina nodded with a smile. "We'd love that."

"We'll see you then." Mrs. Johnson threw her arms around Elaina and embraced her, whispering, "I'm glad we can be friends now."

MONDAY WAS AN EASY day with George no longer on the ranch. The men went to Steven with questions, and there was no one trying to undermine him and his decisions. Sure, there was still some grumbling about doing things differently than they ever had, but nothing like there had been when George was around.

"Looks like the north fence needs mending," Steven remarked, shielding his eyes from the early light. "Storm last week must've been tougher on it than I thought." He shook his head. "I feel like we spend more time fixing fences than we do anything else around here."

Elaina followed his gaze to the crooked wooden posts standing unevenly in the distance. "I'll gather the tools," she offered.

As they worked side by side, the rhythm of hammering nails and the creaks of tightening wire accompanied their conversation. They spoke of mundane tasks at first—the best way to rotate the crops, the need for a new water trough—but gradually, their words took on a more personal hue.

"Back home, I dreamt of land like this," Steven confessed, pausing to wipe sweat from his brow. "Land that stretches as far as the eye can see, where a man can put down roots."

"Roots..." Elaina echoed softly. She had always been rooted to this place. "I used to dream of seeing what lies beyond these fields. But now," she hesitated, glancing at him, "I think there's something to be said for staying put."

Steven met her gaze, and there was an understanding there, a silent acknowledgment of shared dreams.

"Maybe our dreams aren't so different," he said. "You could have sold off the ranch when your father died."

She shook her head. "No, I couldn't. For as long as I can remember, my father would talk to me about how one day his grandchildren would own this ranch. I couldn't disappoint him that way...even after he died."

She watched him then, really looked at him, as they resumed their work. There was a tenderness to his touch as he handled the cattle, a reverence in his voice when he spoke of the soil.

"Your father would be proud," Steven said suddenly, catching her off guard. "You've kept this place going against all odds."

Elaina felt a lump form in her throat. "I hope so. This ranch is my heritage, my past, and future." Her hand brushed against a splintered post, and she recoiled slightly, a small sound of pain escaping her lips.

"Here, let me see." Steven took her hand gently in his, examining the tiny sliver of wood embedded in her skin. His touch was soft, careful as he drew out the splinter. His hazel eyes were filled with concern as he looked up at her. "All better?"

"Yes, thank you," she murmured, acutely aware of the warmth radiating from his hand still enveloping hers. She'd never imagined the man she'd sent for to help her run her ranch would be so...appealing to her.

STEVEN HEAVED THE LAST bale of hay into the loft, muscles aching with the day's labor. As he wiped the sweat from his brow, he noticed a neatly folded cloth on the edge of the loft. Curious, he ambled over and found that it was not just any cloth but a thick blanket protecting a basket. The aroma wafting up to him was unmistakable—beef stew, still warm, accompanied by freshly baked cornbread.

"Elaina," he murmured with a small, appreciative smile. He hadn't made it into the house for lunch that day, instead working on getting the last of the hay into the loft before the rain clouds that were threatening opened up and drenched them. The stew was a sweet gesture. He'd gone without lunch before and would again he was certain. But today he wouldn't have to, and he was thankful for that. He ate quickly and set the basket by the barn door, ready to take to the house when he was finished with the day's work.

Later that week, after a long day mending fences, Steven discovered his favorite shirt hanging on the line, the tear along the seam now expertly stitched. He hadn't even mentioned it to Elaina, yet there it was, mended as if by magic. A tightness in his chest loosened at the realization that she cared enough to tend to such details. His hand lingered on the fabric, tracing the neat stitches, and he felt a surge of gratitude for this extraordinary woman who had come into his life so unexpectedly.

Most days she worked outside with him, but she took care of him when she didn't. She did it in little ways, but he was always appreciative of her efforts.

Steven found Elaina in the barn. Her hair shimmered like spun gold, and her green eyes held flecks of silver in the dim light.

"Care for some company?" he called softly, not wanting to startle her.

"Always," she replied, her voice as soothing as the gentle breeze that whispered through the open barn door. She stood from her task of seeing to bottle feeding one of the calves.

Steven hesitated, then took a step closer to Elaina. Their hands brushed and an electric current passed between them.

"Elaina," he began, his voice barely above a whisper, "may I—"

"Yes," she answered, knowing instinctively what he sought.

Their lips met in a kiss that was both tentative and certain, a promise of something deeper. They pulled away, breathless, their gazes locked in a silent conversation only they could understand.

"Would you dance with me?" Steven asked, heart pounding.

"In here?" Elaina's eyes danced with amusement. "There's no music."

"Then we'll make our own," he said with a grin, offering his hand.

She took it, and they swayed in the moonlit barn, moving to the rhythm of his off-key humming. The world outside faded away, leaving only the sound of their soft laughter and the creaking of old wood beneath their feet.

As the dance ended, they stood forehead to forehead, the connection between them stronger than ever.

He knew from watching his parents that it was never good to let a moment pass that could be spent with the one he cared for. That he loved. Of course, he wasn't ready to say that to Elaina just yet.

ELAINA'S HANDS MOVED with practiced ease, the rough rope slipping through her fingers as she secured the last of the day's hay bales. Steven worked opposite her, his broad back a testament to the labor they'd both grown accustomed to. The air was thick with the scent of rain, and distant thunder murmured like a promise on the horizon.

"Looks like a storm's brewing," Elaina said, glancing out the barn door at the gathering clouds. A drop of sweat trailed down her temple.

"Good for the crops," Steven replied, tying off his bale with a final tug. "Bad for late-night work."

Elaina nodded, swiping her brow with the back of her hand. She couldn't shake the sense of unease that had settled over her. Something felt off, but she could ill afford distractions. The ranch needed every ounce of their attention.

"Let's call it a night after we check on the cattle," she suggested, her voice steady despite the fluttering in her chest.

"Agreed," Steven said. One bad storm could ruin their entire year's worth of income, and they both felt something in the air.

They made their way to the cattle pens, the first fat raindrops pattering against the wooden beams of the barn. They were nearly done for the night when Elaina paused, a frown creasing her forehead.

"Steven, do you smell that?" Her words were snatched away by a gust of wind, but he caught the urgency in her tone.

He sniffed the air, confusion giving way to alarm as the acrid tang of smoke reached him. "Fire!" he shouted.

They rushed outside, the rain now a curtain of water that did little to douse the flames licking hungrily at one corner of the barn. Elaina's heart pounded, the sound drowned out only by the roar of fire and the drumming of the rain.

"Get the calves out!" she yelled, already moving toward the stables. Steven was a stride behind her, his calm demeanor replaced by swift, decisive action as they entered the smoke-filled space.

"Easy, easy," Elaina soothed, her voice a lifeline to the spooked animals. She led the first calf out into the storm, the beast skittish but trusting as they emerged from the barn.

"Elaina! The wind's shifting!" Steven's warning came just as she noticed the change, the fire greedily consuming dry wood and racing along the structure.

"Back to the cows, now!" she commanded, fear lending strength to her limbs. Together, they ran back into the smoky darkness, the heat pressing against them like a physical force.

Their hands found each other in the blackness, fingers intertwining instinctively. "Stay close," Steven breathed, leading the way with a confidence that bolstered Elaina's resolve.

"Always," she replied, her voice a whisper lost in the crackling inferno that raged around them.

The night air cracked with the sound of splintering timber as Elaina and Steven moved through the chaos, a dance of urgency choreographed by necessity. Flames licked hungrily at the edges of the barn, casting wild shadows that transformed the familiar into a realm of danger. The cattle, once docile creatures of routine, now bellowed in distress, their eyes wide and white-rimmed with fear.

"Move them toward the north pasture!" Steven called out, his voice barely audible over the roar of the fire. Elaina nodded, her green eyes reflecting the fiery glow as she swung open the pen gates.

"Come on, " she coaxed, her tone surprisingly steady despite the adrenaline that coursed through her veins. The cows began to shuffle forward, urged by Elaina's gentle shoves and Steven's firm hands guiding them from behind.

Together, they wove through the animals—a strong-willed woman and a dedicated man united by a common goal.

The inferno raged on, devouring the barn as if it were kindling. Sparks flew, carried by the wind, threatening to claim more than just the structure they fought to save. The smoke was thick, stinging their eyes and clawing at their throats, but they pressed on, coughing and gasping for cleaner air.

"Almost there," Elaina panted, her strawberry blonde hair plastered to her forehead with sweat and soot. She glanced back at Steven, who nodded, his blond hair ash-dusted and his hazel eyes focused.

One by one, the cattle spilled out into the open pasture, their moos mingling with the storm's howl. Elaina and Steven worked feverishly to ensure each animal found safety, pushing aside their fears.

With the last cow nudged into the grassy expanse, they took a moment to catch their breath, their backs against the weather-beaten fence. They watched, helpless, as the fire consumed the last of the barn.

"Everything we've built..." Elaina's voice broke.

"We saved the herd, Elaina. We saved what matters most," Steven replied, his hand finding hers amidst the smoldering ruin. His touch brought an unexpected comfort, a silent vow that they would face whatever came next, together.

THE RAIN PATTERED SOFTLY on the charred remains of the barn, its gentle rhythm a stark contrast to the earlier chaos. Elaina's hands trembled as she sifted through the wet ash, her skirts sodden and heavy around her legs. Steven moved beside her, his figure a steady presence in the dimming light.

"Thank God it rained when it did. This fire could have spread to the house or to the pasture. We were lucky, though it doesn't feel like it now."

"Look at us," Elaina murmured, half to herself, "sifting through ruins as if we could piece it all back together with our bare hands."

Steven paused, his gaze meeting hers. "We will rebuild, Elaina. We'll build it stronger, and we won't let this be the end of what you've fought so hard to keep alive."

Their hands touched briefly over a blackened timber, and in that touch lay the promise of renewal.

A glint among the ruins caught Steven's eye. He stooped, plucking a small object from the debris. It was part of a lantern; not one of theirs, he noted, recognizing the make as one sold in town. But more telling was the rag stuffed inside, reeking of kerosene.

"Elaina," he called, and when she joined him, he pointed to the evidence. "This wasn't by chance. This was intentional."

A cold fury settled in Elaina's chest as she took in the makeshift torch. "George," she whispered, the name tasting like bile on her tongue. The pieces fell into place, the subtle manipulations, the veiled threats, and now this—attempted destruction.

"George has been with you for years..." Steven started, but Elaina cut him off.

"Years enough to know just how to hit where it hurts. To think I trusted him, that I..." She shook her head, pushing down the sting of betrayal. "We need to stop him before he tries anything else."

"First light," Steven said, determination in his stance. "We'll deal with George. For now, let's ensure the cattle are secure, and then we rest. We'll need our strength."

ELAINA AND STEVEN, side by side, marched with purpose toward the bunkhouse. They found Beau already awake, his silhouette framed against the flickering light of a lantern inside.

"Beau, we've got to talk," Elaina said, her voice steady despite the tempest raging within.

"Same goes for Nathaniel," Steven added, his gaze meeting Beau's with an unspoken gravity.

The two men emerged, sensing the urgency in their employers' stance. Steven unfurled the charred fabric, evidence of betrayal, and laid bare their plan—a plan that called for both discretion and haste.

"George's treachery ends today," Elaina declared, her green eyes sparking with resolve. "We ride for the sheriff and bring this to light."

Beau nodded, his usual easygoing smile replaced by a grim line. "Count me in," he said, loyalty firm in his tone. Nathaniel simply clapped a hand on Steven's shoulder, a wordless pact sealed between them.

The four mounted their horses and they rode into town.

At the sheriff's office, Elaina's voice didn't waver as she recounted the events, her narrative punctuated by Steven's corroborating details. The sheriff listened, his expression hardening with every word, until the gravity of George's actions was undeniable.

"Justice will be served," the sheriff promised, standing tall, his badge glinting in the morning light. "I'll see to it personally."

With George in custody, the tension that had gripped Elaina's heart began to ease, leaving in its wake a deep-seated determination. She looked over at Steven, his presence a steadfast beacon amidst the maelstrom of emotions.

"Rebuilding won't be easy," she admitted, her voice softer now, touched by an undercurrent of warmth only he could draw forth.

"Nothing worth having ever is," Steven replied.

"Let's go home, Elaina," Steven said, offering his hand.

"Let's go build our life," she responded, taking it without hesitation, her strawberry blonde hair catching the sunlight as she turned to face their destiny, unafraid and united.

Chapter Six

Elaina stood with hands on hips, her strawberry blonde hair pulled back under a wide-brimmed hat, surveying the flurry of activity that had swept over her land. The cowboys, their faces set in lines of determination, had abandoned their usual tasks to take up new roles as they were called on to rebuild the barn.

"Mind that beam, Beau!" she called out, her voice carrying above the cacophony. Beau, tall and lanky, waved an acknowledgment from atop the skeletal frame of the new barn, his sandy hair plastered to his forehead with sweat.

"Will do, ma'am!" he replied.

Steven was in the middle of the fray, his strong arms pounding in nails. He called out commands to the other men, and everyone obeyed instantly. Even the cowboys who had remained loyal to George were disgusted with the older man's actions, and they were doing all they could to make up for their short-sightedness in following him.

"Never seen anything come together this quick," Steven said, pride edging his voice. "It's like the whole valley's come alive to help."

Elaina followed his gaze to where the Johnsons' wagon rolled into view, rousing a cheer from the workers. The neighboring family had heard of the fire that claimed the old barn and, true to the spirit of frontier kinship, had brought their own ranch hands to aid in the effort.

"Looks like we've got more willing hands," Elaina noted, her lips curving upwards. The despair that had gripped her heart when flames devoured her father's legacy was now giving way to something warmer, something akin to hope.

"More mouths to feed, too," Steven said, but his tone was light, teasing. "Good thing they're bringing some provisions."

"We'll have this done in no time," Mr. Johnson called.

"Thank you!" Elaina responded, her gratitude genuine.

As the day wore on, the sun climbed higher, casting a golden glow over the burgeoning structure. Elaina couldn't help but marvel at how quickly despair could turn to hope with the help of friends and neighbors. She thought of her father and wondered how many times he'd seen the community coming together in such a way.

"Looks like it's going to be bigger than the last one," Nathaniel commented, wiping his brow with a bandana as he joined them. His quiet strength had been a cornerstone during the rebuilding, just as it had been in the daily grind of ranch life. Elaina hadn't realized what a genuinely good man she had working for her until Steven had come along.

"Stronger, too," Steven added.

She smiled as she watched her husband, working with the men as well as leading them. It wasn't just the barn that was being rebuilt, but also the trust and dependence between them, woven tight like the joints and beams of the structure before them.

"By the end of the day, I reckon we'll have a roof over it," Nathaniel said, squinting up at the sky.

"And not a moment too soon," Elaina murmured. But even the threat of a storm seemed diminished in the face of their collective resolve.

Steven nodded, looking at the storm clouds. "Every nail, every board...it's a step closer to what we lost."

"More than that," Elaina replied, watching him rejoin the men. "It's a step toward everything we stand to gain."

ELAINA'S HANDS MOVED deftly, carving generous slices of meat from the freshly butchered steer. Cynthia worked beside her, seasoning the cuts while Mrs. Johnson—Cheryl—tended to a pot bubbling over an open fire.

"Pass me that platter, dear," Cheryl said, her voice as warm as the midday sun. Elaina complied, offering a smile as the older woman piled it high with steaming potatoes. Together, they filled plates and carried them to the long table set up under the newly erected awning.

"Get it while it's hot!" Cynthia called. The men gathered like bees to honey, crowding around the makeshift buffet with a chorus of thanks and hungry bellies.

Steven stood back for a moment, watching Elaina as she served the cowboys. Her strawberry blonde hair had escaped its ties, framing her face in wild waves, and there was a smudge of dirt on her cheek that only made her piercing green eyes stand out more.

"Make sure you eat something too," he reminded her as he finally stepped forward to take his plate.

"Only after everyone else has had their fill," Elaina replied. So much of the work being done was not being paid for, and it was the least she could do to make sure their bellies were filled.

After the meal, the last beams were hoisted, the final nails were driven home, and finally, the barn stood completed.

"Stronger than before," Steven murmured, his gaze tracing the lines of the structure they'd all poured their sweat into.

"More than just wood and nails," Elaina agreed, standing beside him. A gentle breeze stirred her hair, carrying with it the freshness of the coming night.

They surveyed the barn together. There was a sense of renewal here, a new beginning as they took the ranch from under George's control. As they stood shoulder to shoulder, the unspoken bond between them was palpable—their marriage was becoming something real and not just an agreement between two people to help one another where they could.

"It'll do well against the storms," she observed, her voice carrying a hint of pride.

"Against anything," Steven added.

ELAINA PULLED HER GLOVES tighter, the leather worn from days of labor. Steven's broad back was a steady presence beside her as they ushered the last of the calves into the new barn. The sun hung low in the sky, casting long shadows that stretched across the golden hay scattered on the ground.

"Come on, little ones," she coaxed, patting the rump of a particularly stubborn calf. The animal bawled but finally moved forward, following its companions into the spacious enclosure.

"Looks like they approve," Steven said with a chuckle, wiping sweat from his brow. His shirt clung to his body, outlining the muscles honed by years of physical labor.

Elaina nodded, watching the calves explore their new surroundings. It was true; they had lost income from the fire that had ravaged the old barn—a setback that would pinch come winter. But as she looked around, counting the heads of each calf, a swell of gratitude replaced her worry. Every single animal was accounted for, and not a soul had been harmed in the blaze.

"We're blessed," she whispered, more to herself than to Steven. Even with the financial loss, they still had their health, their land, and each other.

"Indeed, we are," he agreed, catching her eye.

Once the animals were all where they should be, they made their way back to the main house, dust clinging to their boots. Inside, the simple wooden structure felt like a sanctuary after the week's turmoil.

Steven lit the oil lamp on the dining table, its glow filling the room with a soft light. Elaina sank into a chair, exhaustion seeping into her bones, yet she couldn't help but feel content.

"Could've been so much worse," Steven mused.

"Could have," she agreed. "But it wasn't. And look at what we accomplished." She gestured toward the window where the outline of the new barn was visible.

"More than I ever did back East," he said with a humble nod. "Feels like...we're building something lasting."

"Something ours," Elaina added, her heart swelling with a sense of partnership that went beyond contracts and agreements.

Elaina stood in the modest kitchen, a frown creasing her brow as she poked at the blackened contents of the skillet. The steak was beyond redemption, looking more like a piece of charcoal than a meal. She shook her head, muttering under her breath about her lack of culinary finesse. Cynthia, who had been working tirelessly since the fire, had finally taken a well-deserved evening off, leaving Elaina to manage the stove.

"Smells like...dinner's ready?" Steven's voice held a teasing note as he leaned against the doorway, observing the scene. Now he understood why Elaina had never cooked for him before. She simply didn't know how!

"Ready as it'll ever be," Elaina replied with a resigned sigh, plating the sad excuse for supper. Her green eyes met his, and she couldn't help but let out a small, self-deprecating laugh. "I'm afraid you're in for quite the feast."

Steven took the plate from her hands, examining the charred steak with an amused expression. "Well, I've heard tell that char adds flavor." He cut into it with exaggerated care, bringing a piece to his mouth and chewing thoughtfully. "Mmm, robust," he declared, his eyes twinkling as he swallowed.

Elaina leaned back against the counter, arms folded, watching him eat what she considered a culinary disaster. "You don't have to pretend it's good on my account," she said, the corners of her mouth twitching upward. "Cynthia tried to teach me to cook, but I just never had the knack for it."

"Elaina, I've eaten meals that were burnt worse than this as my sisters learned to cook. Besides, I didn't marry you for your cooking." He winked at her, setting the fork down.

"Good thing, too," she chuckled, her spirit unbruised by the mishap. "I reckon I'm better suited for rounding up cattle and mending fences than I am for this." She gestured toward the stove with a playful roll of her eyes.

"That you are," he agreed, stepping closer. "And speaking of mending, that blue dress you fixed up last week—never seen finer stitches. You have a real talent, Elaina."

Her cheeks warmed at the compliment. "Thank you, Steven. It's something I can control, unlike this..." She waved her hand over the dinner table, where the scorched meal lay in defeat.

"Control isn't everything," he murmured, taking her hand in his. "Sometimes, it's the unexpected things that bring the most joy." His thumb brushed gently over her knuckles, a comforting touch that spoke volumes of their growing bond.

They shared a quiet moment, and Elaina felt the weight of the week's struggles lift, replaced by a sense of camaraderie and hope for their future together on the ranch.

Steven's calloused fingers traced the line of Elaina's jaw, a gentle caress that belied the strength in his hands—hands that had rebuilt her father's barn, that had held her when the night brought doubts instead of dreams. She leaned into his touch, her skin tingling with an anticipation that was new and yet as old as the hills that cradled their ranch.

"Elaina," he whispered.

She nodded, her breath catching in her throat. Words were unnecessary.

With careful reverence, Steven brushed stray strands of strawberry-blonde hair from her face, tucking them behind her ear. She closed her eyes, savoring the simple intimacy, feeling the last remnants of the day's troubles melt away under his touch.

Their movements were unhurried, a slow dance guided by the rhythm of their hearts. Clothing fell away like leaves in autumn, revealing the soft contours of Elaina's body, the sculpted lines of his.

The world outside faded to nothing—the charred remains of the past, the uncertainty of tomorrow—they all slipped away as Steven and Elaina rediscovered each other.

His lips explored her body, and she arched into him, thankful that she'd found a man who was not only good for the ranch but good for her. He was everything she'd ever hoped to find in a husband, and she was thankful for every moment they had together.

With every touch, every kiss, every shared breath, they felt the rebirth of their land, their home. The new barn stood solid and proud in the moonlight.

As she lay in his arms before falling asleep, Elaina knew there would be many more obstacles in their lives, but she was sure that with Steven by her side, they could overcome them all.

Chapter Seven

The church bell's final chime lingered as Elaina stepped outside into the crisp autumn air. The fabric of her Sunday dress brushed against her ankles as she navigated through the dispersing congregation, her green eyes seeking the familiar form of her husband.

"Steven," she called out gently, once she had found him speaking with some of the townsmen by the hitching post.

He turned at the sound of her voice. "Elaina, everything all right?" Steven asked, excusing himself from the other men with a courteous nod.

"Can we walk a while?" Her words were soft but deliberate, and he immediately gave her his full attention.

They strolled, side by side, down the dirt path that led away from the churchyard.

"Steven, there's something you need to know," Elaina began, her fingers worrying the hem of her sleeve. "I've been wanting to tell you all week, but I needed to be sure."

He stopped walking, turning to face her fully, his expression open and attentive.

"I'm expecting," she said. "We're going to have a baby."

For a heartbeat, the world seemed to pause. Then, Steven's face broke into a wide, unabashed grin—the kind of smile that could only be described as youthful joy etched onto the rugged landscape of a man's face.

"Elaina, that is...that's wonderful news!" His hands reached for hers, engulfing them in warmth. "You are going to be an incredible mother."

Her heart swelled, but with it came a tide of protective instincts. "I want to—no, I need to step back from the ranch work, Steven. With the baby...I can't risk it. I worry I'll get kicked or have a bad fall and lose the baby."

He nodded. "Of course, you're right. You shouldn't be out there with the men, not now." He tucked a stray lock of her hair behind her ear. "From now on, your job is inside, taking care of yourself and our little one. I'll handle everything outside with the crew."

"Are you sure? Can the ranch run without both of us out there?" Doubt edged her words.

"Elaina," he said, his voice low and steady, "the ranch will survive. But you and our child are my priority. We're a team, and right now, this is how we protect our future—all three of us."

She studied his face and felt a wave of gratitude wash over her. This man, who had come from so far to stand beside her, now promised to shoulder the weight of their shared dream.

"Thank you, Steven," she whispered, allowing herself to lean into his strength for just a moment. It would be hard for her to let him take on the added duties, but their baby needed to be her first concern.

ELAINA'S FINGERS SIFTED through the flour, a fine dusting settling on the kitchen table like the first whisper of snow. The morning sun filtered through the window, casting a warm glow on Cynthia's patient smile as she guided Elaina's hands through the motions of kneading the dough.

"Like this," Cynthia encouraged, her voice a gentle melody against the rhythmic thud of dough on wood. "You'll feel it become ready under your palms."

Elaina tried to mimic her friend's expertise, her brow furrowed in concentration. They had started at dawn and now the clock hands pointed accusingly toward late afternoon.

"Maybe we should've started with something simpler," Elaina sighed, wiping a strand of strawberry blonde hair from her face with the back of her flour-dusted hand.

Cynthia chuckled, shaking her head. "Bread is simple, once you get the hang of it. And besides, Steven will love it because you made it."

Elaina wanted so desperately to master these domestic arts, to fill their home with the kind of comfort and nourishment she imagined a wife should provide.

By the time Steven's shadow darkened the doorway, the kitchen was a battlefield of culinary mishaps. Loaves lay slumped on cooling racks, their crusts too hard or innards too doughy. Elaina's apron was smeared with evidence of her efforts, and the chickens outside clucked contentedly, well-fed on her failures.

Steven paused at the sight of her, his eyes searching hers as he took in the scene. He removed his hat as he studied the scene, scratching his head in confusion.

"Elaina, what's all this?" His voice held a hint of bewildered amusement.

She couldn't hold back the tears that sprang forth, drops of frustration and disappointment that she hastily tried to hide. "I wanted to learn to cook…for you. But everything's been a disaster. I can't seem to do anything right in this kitchen."

Steven crossed the room in a few long strides, enveloping her in his arms. He drew her close, his embrace a fortress against her self-doubt.

"Hey now," he whispered. "You don't have to be perfect at everything. You're learning, and that's what matters. We've got a lifetime for you to try again."

A sigh escaped her, her body relaxing against his sturdy form. In his arms, she found the strength to let go of her insecurities.

"Thank you," she murmured, the words barely audible over the steady thrum of his heart. "For understanding."

"I always will," he promised, sealing the vow with a kiss atop her head.

ELAINA STOOD AT THE threshold of their modest homestead, the evening air crisp with the scent of the coming autumn. Her hands were still dusted with flour, remnants of her futile attempt at becoming the cook she felt Steven deserved. She watched him as he approached.

"Elaina," Steven began, his voice imbued with warmth as he took in her downcast eyes, "I need you to understand something." He reached for her hands, brushing away the white powder with gentle strokes. "I didn't marry you for your cooking skills or how well you can manage chores."

She looked up, meeting his hazel gaze that seemed to look right through her, seeing all the doubts that lingered unspoken. His thumb caressed the back of her hand, a simple touch that spoke volumes.

"I married you for who you are, for the partnership we could have on this land." His words unwound the tight knot of worry in her chest. "We'll get through whatever comes our way, together."

It was a good thing he hadn't married her for her cooking skills. He'd have left long before. Of course, the truth was, he'd married her for her land. She just hoped the land was enough to keep them together.

Steven followed her gaze toward the barn where bales of hay were stored high against the wooden beams. Their hard work was evident in the stockpile they had accumulated over the long summer days.

"Albert, Nathaniel, Beau, and I, we've put in a good supply of hay," he reassured her. "But I won't lie to you; I still worry there might not be enough for winter."

Her heart clenched at his honesty, knowing well the unpredictability of the seasons. "Then we will find a way," Elaina said. "We always do."

"That we do," Steven agreed, pulling her closer against him.

ELAINA WATCHED OUT the window as Steven slipped quietly into the barn. It was not the first time she'd seen him vanish into the wooden structure at odd hours. Her hands stilled their work on the dough, flour dusting her apron like a light snowfall.

"Steven," she called earlier that day when she caught him heading out with a determined stride, "where are you off to?"

"Ah, just some chores," he replied.

"Chores?" There was a tremor in her voice, a note of uncertainty that she despised but couldn't quite hide. The ranch had settled into a rhythm under his careful management, and yet, instead of relief, a new kind of worry gnawed at her.

"Nothing for you to fret about, Elaina," Steven said. "You just focus on staying well, all right?"

She wrapped her arms around herself, feeling a chill that owed nothing to the cool breeze wafting through the open window. Was it possible that now, with the ranch thriving and their future seemingly secured, he found little need for her companionship? The thought pierced her with a silent dread.

She wiped her hands on her apron and made her way to the door. Elaina's heart ached with a longing for understanding, for connection. They had built a life together out of necessity, but she wanted so much more from their marriage than she'd imagined when she'd sent a letter off to an unknown matchmaker.

"Can our marriage last if we no longer need to be together for the ranch?" she whispered.

Determined to shake off the unease, Elaina returned to the kitchen, her fingers resuming their dance across the dough. The bread would be ready by morning, and this time it would turn out. It had taken her a week, but she'd mastered the simple task of breadmaking.

Outside, the barn loft held a secret project cradled in the glow of a lantern—a cradle taking shape beneath Steven's skilled hands. He wanted to present it to her for their first Christmas together.

SNOWFLAKES DESCENDED upon the ranch with a silent ferocity that seemed almost personal in its intent. Elaina watched from the window of their small but sturdy home, the world outside rapidly succumbing to a blanket of white. The early blizzard had come without warning, swallowing the horizon and hurling the ranch into an unexpected solitude.

Inside, she built the fire to stay warm, but she worried that Steven was out in the snow. Had he gotten to shelter before the snow had blinded him? Elaina drew her shawl tighter around her shoulders. She was confined, a prisoner of the storm, her only company Cynthia, and her cooking lessons.

"Elaina?" Cynthia's voice was soft but infused with warmth.

"Here, by the window," Elaina replied, her voice steady but laced with the unspoken worry for Steven and the men out in the storm, fighting to shield the cattle from nature's wrath.

With careful steps, Cynthia joined her by the window, her blue eyes wide with concern. "The bread won't bake itself," she offered gently, nudging Elaina toward the kitchen. "Let's get your hands busy. It'll help pass the time."

Elaina nodded and allowed herself to be led to the kitchen. Over the next three days, the storm raged on, but so did life within the house.

They measured and mixed, the scent of baking bread bravely battling the cold that sought to invade their sanctuary.

WHEN THE SKIES EVENTUALLY cleared, revealing a landscape transformed and glittering beneath the sun's tentative touch, Elaina wrapped herself in her coat and ventured out. The air was sharp, biting at her cheeks.

Her breath formed clouds before her as she made her way across the thawing ground to visit Cheryl. The walk was harder than usual, the snow resisting each step, but Elaina was determined to visit her friend.

"Cheryl," Elaina greeted as her friend opened the door.

"Elaina! Come in, come in! I feared you'd been buried under a drift!" Cheryl exclaimed.

They settled into comfortable chairs, and Elaina took a deep breath, savoring the sense of normalcy that the room offered. "I'm expecting," she said, the words tumbling out with a mixture of excitement and trepidation.

"Truly? Oh, Elaina, that's wonderful news!" Cheryl beamed, her happiness genuine and contagious.

Elaina smiled, a soft, uncertain smile. "It is... and yet, everything feels so different now. This land, this life we've built—it all has new meaning." She glanced down at her hands and then back up at Cheryl, whose eyes glowed with understanding.

"Change can be frightening, but it can also bring about the most beautiful things," Cheryl replied, reaching out to take Elaina's hand. "You're creating a life, a family. That's a powerful thing."

And so, they spoke of the future, of children and dreams, while the last remnants of the storm melted away outside.

ELAINA WRAPPED HER shawl tighter around her shoulders as she stepped out onto the porch, where Steven stood waiting, his gaze fixed on the horizon where the land stretched endlessly.

"Walk with me?" he asked, extending his arm with a gentle smile.

Elaina nodded, slipping her hand into the crook of his elbow. Together, they strolled along the path that snaked through the ranch, the silence between them comfortable.

As they passed the barn, Steven's steps slowed, and he gestured toward the open fields beyond. "In the spring, I want to expand our stock," he said, his voice carrying the weight of careful consideration. "I've been thinking about sheep. They're hardy, good for wool and meat."

Elaina glanced at him, noting the earnestness in his tone. "Sheep?" she echoed, her brow furrowing slightly. The concept was foreign to her, yet the way Steven spoke of it made it sound like an essential piece of their future.

"Yep," he affirmed with a nod. "They'll be good for the ranch, and our children will inherit a thriving operation. It's important to me that we build something lasting here."

"Children..." she murmured. Yet, as she looked up at Steven doubt crept into her heart. Was it truly the legacy he cared for, or was it her? She searched his face for signs of affection, for any hint that his feelings went beyond the bounds of their practical arrangement.

"Steven," she began, her voice barely above a whisper, "do you ever think about...us? Beyond the ranch, I mean."

He stopped then, turning to face her fully. His expression was one of surprise. "Elaina," he said softly, reaching out to cup her cheek. "This ranch—it's not just land and animals to me. It's a home. Our home. And you, you're the heart of it all."

She wanted to believe him, to see in his eyes the love she so desperately craved, but her insecurities clouded her judgment. She felt his thumb gently stroke her cheek, and she leaned into his touch, yearning for more than words.

"Everything I do here, every decision I make—it's for our future, for your happiness," he continued. "I may not say it much, but I care for you, Elaina. More than I've ever cared for the land."

Elaina's eyes welled with tears, the emotion in his voice resonating deep within her. But still, the nagging thought that she was merely a means to an end persisted, casting a shadow over her heart.

"Thank you, Steven. That means a lot to hear," she managed to say, though her voice trembled with uncertainty.

They resumed walking, the land around them coming alive with the promise of new growth. Steven pointed out where the sheep would graze, his plans meticulous and full of hope. She listened, but her heart wasn't eased. The land was what he wanted. Not her.

Chapter Eight

Elaina stood at the counter, her hands dusted with flour as she kneaded the dough. The kitchen was warm from the heat of the wood stove, the scent of baking bread mingling with the earthy aroma of stew simmering over the fire. It was a simple meal, yet Elaina felt a swell of pride at being able to prepare it without assistance.

"Looks like you've got the hang of it," Cynthia said as she wiped down the already immaculate table.

Elaina glanced over her shoulder, her lips curving into a small smile. "I suppose I do. At least Steven won't go hungry." Learning to cook had been so much harder than anything else she'd ever done, but she was very proud of her accomplishment.

As the dough settled under her palms, Elaina's thoughts wandered to Steven, working tirelessly in the fields. She imagined his contentment when he would come in to find a hot meal waiting, something she had prepared herself. It was a comfort, a way to show her care.

Cynthia moved about the room, her movements graceful and quiet as she took on tasks that had become increasingly cumbersome for Elaina. With the baby growing each day, even the simplest of chores seemed to require a great deal of effort. But Cynthia never complained, always stepping in with a helping hand or a kind word.

"Let me get that," Cynthia offered as Elaina reached up to place a jar back on the shelf, her rounded belly making the stretch uncomfortable.

"Thank you," Elaina replied, accepting the help with a grateful nod. She hated needing assistance, but she recognized the necessity of it.

"Anything else you need?" Cynthia asked.

"Just your company," Elaina said, and meant it. They shared a companionable silence, broken only by the occasional crackle from the stove and the rhythmic thud of dough against the countertop.

When the bread finally went into the oven and the stew was left to simmer, Elaina sank into a chair with a weary sigh. Her body ached in new ways, a constant reminder of the life she carried within.

Cynthia sat across from her, sewing a small garment for the baby, her needle darting in and out of the fabric with skilled precision. Elaina watched her for a moment, thinking how fortunate she was to have such a friend in these uncertain times.

"Thank you, Cynthia," Elaina said softly, her gratitude spilling over. "For everything."

"It's what you pay me for," Cynthia replied. "Not that I wouldn't do it just for a friend, and you are my closest friend. Speaking of which…"

"What?" Elaina asked. "Are you hiding something from me?"

"Not deliberately…" Cynthia took a deep breath. "I'm going to supper at the diner in town with Nathaniel tonight."

"Nathaniel?" Elaina asked, looking at her friend. "Our ranch hand?"

Cynthia nodded. "Yes. He asked me if I'd go with him a month ago, and I told him we had to wait. I didn't want to go before you could cook a meal on your own, but now that you can…"

"Oh, that's wonderful!" Elaina said. "He's a good man!"

"I agree. After Lance died, I didn't think I'd ever be interested in a man again, but I'm still young, and I think Nathaniel is the man to change my mind."

"I will need all the details tomorrow," Elaina said, smiling. "I can make stew and bread every night if that's what it takes to help you find love again."

Cynthia blushed but nodded. "I'll be here when you need me, but…I hope something will come of this with Nathaniel."

"I hope so too!"

ELAINA CAREFULLY PLACED the last fork beside the porcelain plate, her movements deliberate but growing steadier with each passing day. The aroma of roasted chicken mingled with the scent of fresh-baked bread, wafting through the modest dining room of the ranch house. As Steven entered, he paused, inhaling deeply, a look of genuine appreciation lighting up his hazel eyes.

"Smells like heaven in here," he remarked, pulling out the chair across from Elaina and taking his seat.

"Thank you," Elaina replied, her cheeks flushed with a mixture of pride and the warmth from the stove where she had labored. "I made this meal completely by myself without Cynthia even watching me."

Steven looked up from his plate, his gaze meeting hers with an unmistakable gleam of admiration. "It looks good. And it's delicious," he said, after taking a generous bite of the chicken, which fell apart under the gentle pressure of his fork.

She watched him eat, her heart swelling with a sense of accomplishment she hadn't felt in a long time. "I'm so glad you like it."

As they ate, the conversation drifted naturally to the upcoming holiday season. "Back in Massachusetts, we had quite the traditions for Christmas," Steven began, a nostalgic smile playing on his lips. "We'd decorate the whole house with holly and ivy, and my father would cut down a tree from our woods. We'd spend the evening stringing popcorn and cranberries to hang on it."

"That sounds lovely," Elaina mused, picturing the scene in her mind. "My family was simpler in celebration, but one thing we never missed was making a wreath from the evergreens around our property. My father would lift me onto his shoulders so I could place it right above the door. I miss that."

They continued to share stories, the threads of their past weaving together to form the tapestry of a shared future.

"Perhaps this year, we can blend our traditions," Elaina suggested. "Create new ones for our own little family."

Steven reached across the table, his hand covering hers, rough and warm. "I'd like that very much," he said.

After supper, they moved to the small living area, and he brought up the holidays once again. "Elaina," Steven began, the firelight casting shadows across his strong features as he turned toward her. "I've been thinking about Christmas coming up. Makes me wish you could meet my family back in Massachusetts."

His voice held a wistful note, and she tilted her head, curious. Steven spoke often of the ranch, the cattle, and the land, but mentions of his family were few and far between.

"Your mother," she ventured, "what's she like?"

A fond smile tugged at the corners of his mouth. "Strong, like you. She'd take to you straight away—I'm sure of it. Her heart's big enough for the whole town."

Elaina nodded, a warmth spreading through her chest that had little to do with the fire before her. It was a connection, however distant, to the man who sat beside her.

"Tell me more about your siblings," she said, eager to know the people who had shaped the man she married.

Steven chuckled, a sound that rumbled deep in his chest. "Well, we were quite the brood—sixteen of us—and all but the oldest four had a penchant for mischief." He leaned back, his gaze growing distant as if he could see the rolling hills of his childhood right there in the flickering flames. "There was this one time we painted the neighbor's horse bright blue. Nearly gave the poor man a heart attack."

Elaina's laughter filled the room, clear and genuine. "Blue?"

"Blue as the summer sky," he confirmed with a nod. "Took weeks to wash out. And then there was the incident with the apple pies... Ma was making pies for a church bake sale, and my brother and I replaced all the sugar with salt. The church was trying to raise money to pay for new windows, and we liked the old ones."

She listened, laughing at the tales of youthful rebellion, each story painting a picture of a life so different from her own, yet somehow familiar in its undercurrents of love and camaraderie. Steven's family, it seemed, had been a force to be reckoned with, and she could easily imagine him as the ringleader of such chaos. "Were you the oldest?"

He shook his head. "No, I was third from the youngest."

As he recounted the tales, his face animated with the retelling, Elaina saw past the broad shoulders and the strength they promised. She saw the boy who had never truly left the man—he was still so amused with his youthful pranks.

"Sounds like you were quite the hellions," she finally said, the word feeling strange yet fitting on her tongue.

"We were," he admitted, his hazel eyes meeting hers. "But we looked out for each other. Always. That's why when a letter asking for a groom arrived at my sister's house, she sent me." He shook his head. "I hope our children have that type of loyalty for one another—the kind I have for my siblings, and you."

"Thank you," she whispered, not entirely sure what she was thanking him for—the stories, the honesty, or perhaps the hope that their child would know such bonds.

"Always," Steven said, knowing it was true.

"Steven," she began, her voice steady but laced with a hint of nostalgia, "my father raised me with a firm hand. He believed that discipline and hard work were the cornerstone of character." She paused, her piercing green eyes searching his face for understanding. "I think I want our children to know that same strength."

Steven nodded. "I respect that, Elaina," he replied, his voice carrying the calm assurance that had first drawn her to him. "It's important, raising kids with a sense of right and wrong. Means they won't have to wander far to find themselves—or a spouse—when it's time." He shook his head. "Only two of our family were able to stay in the same area to marry. Our reputation as the 'demon horde' had everyone in the area reluctant to allow their children to marry into our family."

The corners of her mouth turned up in a small smile, relief flowing through her at his agreement. It was one thing to marry out of necessity, another to find common ground where it truly mattered.

Just then, Steven stood and strode across the room with purpose, revealing a large, wrapped object that had been hidden behind the settee. Elaina watched as he carefully unwrapped a phonograph.

"Remember that night we danced in the barn?" he asked, a boyish grin spreading across his face.

Elaina nodded, feeling a warmth that wasn't from the fire.

"Well," Steven continued as he placed a round disk on the turntable, "I thought it was high time we danced to some actual music." His fingers were gentle, yet assured, as he wound up the phonograph and set the needle down with a soft crackle.

Music blossomed into the room, a lilting waltz that felt both foreign and familiar. Steven extended his hand to her, an unspoken invitation hanging in the air as the music wove its spell.

Elaina rose and took his hand. They found their stance, close enough to feel each other's breaths. As the first notes enveloped them, they began to move, slowly at first, then with more confidence.

Elaina stumbled slightly, her foot catching on the hem of her skirt as Steven's hand steadied her with a firm grip. A laugh bubbled up from her throat, unfurling in the warm air of the parlor as they clumsily found their rhythm once again. Neither was a particularly good dancer, and their constant missteps caused them to laugh at themselves constantly.

"Mercy, I never knew two left feet could be such good company," Elaina teased.

"Seems to me we're both guilty of that," Steven replied. "But I reckon it's more about who you're stepping on than how well you move."

The needle on the phonograph crackled and popped. They spun, tripped, and laughed again, the melody forgiving their missteps as if this dance was crafted just for them—their imperfect ballet.

As the hour wore on and their laughter subsided, their movements became less about the dance and more about the closeness it brought. Breathless, Elaina rested her head against Steven's broad chest, listening to the steady beat of his heart mingling with the fading waltz.

"Steven," she began, "when our child comes into this world, I want them to know every day just how cherished they are."

"Yes," he agreed, his voice low and resonant. "We'll raise them to know they're loved unconditionally. I'll dance with all the girls, and you dance with all the boys."

"Just how many children do you think we're having?" she asked in mock dismay.

"Three or four dozen. No more than that."

She laughed. "I don't know...that sounds like an awful lot to me. Remember, I was an only child."

"And you missed knowing that having siblings is one of the best things in the world. Think of all the mischief you and your imaginary siblings could have gotten into!"

She shook her head. "I don't know about that. I don't want to be the mother of a group of hellions."

"That's where raising them with strict rules comes into play. I'll teach them to only prank each other and not throw apples at all the townspeople."

"Just promise me you'll love them, and I think we'll be good."

"Exactly," Steven murmured, leaning down to press a kiss to her forehead. "Our little ones will never doubt their place in this world or in our hearts."

Elaina moved back to her rocking chair, picking up the afghan she was crocheting for the baby. "I almost wish the baby would be here before Christmas," she said softly. "I want to make presents for him or her."

"Christmas," Steven said, leaning back in his chair. "It always smelled of gingerbread at my ma's house. She had a knack for baking them just right—crisp edges with chewy centers."

A smile tugged at Elaina's lips, imagining a kitchen filled with the sweet, spicy scent of festive treats. "Gingerbread, huh?" she asked. She'd never equated gingerbread with Christmas, but if he did, she would make the most of it.

"Yep. Never was Christmas without them. Ma said it was like bringing warmth into the home—something about how the molasses and spices mixed to create something almost magical."

She nodded, picturing the scene—a bustling kitchen, laughter hanging in the air, the rich aroma enveloping the family. "I think I could give it a try," Elaina said, more to herself than to him. "Cynthia's got a hand for baking. She could show me how."

"Would you do that?" He looked genuinely touched, and it stirred something within her—the desire to bring that piece of his past into their present.

"Of course." Determination settled in her chest. "I want our child to have those kinds of memories, too. To know the warmth of traditions."

"Elaina, that'd mean the world to me," he replied, his voice thick with an emotion he seldom showed. He shook his head. "At times the girls would work together and build a house from gingerbread while we were out working on fences. We'd get in at the end of a day in the snow, and there would be hot chocolate and a gingerbread house, along with all the men and women they'd decorated. I was always the first to steal a piece of the roof...usually the chimney. My youngest sister, Ida Mae, would get so mad at me. The sister between us, Joy, would have to quiet her down. Of course, Joy could make anyone happy. Ma gave her the name that suited her perfectly."

"Steven," she said, unable to meet his gaze as she spoke her fears, "I'm not like other women...I've spent so much time being strong, being...mannish. Am I enough?" When he spoke of his sisters, he always talked about them as if they grew up with a mixing spoon in their hands and covered in flour as they learned to cook and do all the wifely tasks. She felt inept.

"Elaina," he said firmly, lifting her chin gently so their eyes met. "You're exactly who I need. You're fierce, brave, and caring. And I don't want anyone else by my side. I vowed to protect you, and I meant every word."

His touch was tender, a stark contrast to the calloused hands of a man who worked the land. She covered his hands with hers, thankful that he was willing to say all the right things, even if he didn't mean them.

Chapter Nine

Steven and Elaina readied themselves for the journey to Billings. The sleigh was hitched up, and they had baked potatoes at their feet to keep them warm. They could eat them on the way home if they became hungry.

"Ready?" Steven asked, his voice steady as always, though Elaina noticed a slight tightening around his eyes—the only indicator of the tension he felt about the trial ahead.

"Let's get this done," she replied as she climbed into the sleigh beside him.

The journey was quiet, the only sounds were the crunch of snow beneath the runners and the occasional snort from the horses. All she could think about was what the trial would hold. What if they didn't find George guilty?

They arrived at the courthouse just as the town clock struck nine, its bell echoing through the chilled air. Inside, the wooden benches were filled with people who turned to watch as Elaina and Steven entered. The bailiff called the room to order, and George was led in, handcuffs clinking. His steely blue eyes found Elaina's, but she met his gaze with an unyielding glare.

When called upon, Elaina took the stand, her voice clear and strong as she recounted the betrayal, the faked numbers, and the missing funds. Steven followed, his testimony delivered with a calm certainty that left no room for doubt. They were a united front, both needing justice.

The gavel sounded with a finality as the judge declared George guilty. He was to be sentenced to prison, his ill-gotten gains to be returned, and restitution made for the barn he had burned down. Relief washed over Elaina in waves, and she reached for Steven's hand, squeezing it tightly as they listened to the sentence being handed down.

"Thank you," she murmured to him as they stood to leave the courtroom, the weight of the past months lifting with each step they took toward the doors.

Steven nodded. "It's a new beginning for us, for the ranch."

The world outside was a pristine white canvas, the snow muffling the sounds of the sleigh's runners as they cut through the fresh powder. Elaina nestled closer to Steven for warmth, her breath visible in the crisp air.

"Can you believe it, Steven? After all this time, we're finally free of this whole mess," she said.

Steven's strong hands held the reins steady, his gaze fixed on the path ahead. He then turned toward her, his hazel eyes alive with the same excitement that danced in hers. "It's more than I dared hope for," he admitted. "Now we can think about the future—the ranch's future."

The sleigh glided over a small rise, and she felt as though they were being carried along by the winds of fortune.

"Have you thought about what we'll do with the money, once we get it back?" she asked.

"Actually, I have." Steven's voice held a hint of something new, a flicker of plans forming. "I've been thinking...maybe it's time we expand the operations. Build a separate barn for the sheep I've been wanting to raise."

"Really?" Elaina turned to him, considering the suggestion. It was an ambitious dream, but one well within reach given their recent stroke of luck.

"Think about it, Elaina. Sheep are hardy. They'll do well here, and the wool could open new trade opportunities for us. Not to mention the meat will fetch a good price at market."

She looked out across the fields blanketed in snow, envisioning the pastures come spring, dotted with grazing sheep. It was a prospect that warmed her from the inside out, a tangible manifestation of the hope and determination that had carried them through the hardest of times.

"Yes," she breathed out, the word carrying with it all the promise of a shared future. "Yes, let's do that."

"Steven," Elaina began, "have you noticed how Cynthia and Nathaniel are when they're together?" Her voice was thoughtful.

Steven turned to her. "I have," he replied.

"Mmm." She nodded, a plan blossoming in her mind. "I've been thinking—perhaps it's time we give Nathaniel more responsibility. Make him foreman?"

"Foreman, huh?" Steven mused. "He's got the respect of the men, and he's fair. It makes sense."

"And—" She hesitated for a moment, a boldness creeping into her tone. "We could build them a cabin, here on the ranch, close to the main house. It would be good for them...for all of us."

Steven's nod was slow but decisive. "I like that," he said. "It'd make this place feel even more like a family."

Elaina smiled. She liked the idea of no longer sharing their house with Cynthia and having more privacy, but she knew she needed the other woman close by.

When they were finally home, Elaina excused herself and retreated to the parlor where her knitting awaited her. The fire crackled in the hearth, its glow illuminating the room with an amber light that danced across the walls. She settled onto the plush settee, her fingers deftly picking up the half-finished sock she'd been crafting for Steven.

As Christmas approached, the urgency to complete the hand-knit set gripped her—a scarf, gloves, and now the socks. The soft wool slipped between her fingers, the repetitive motion soothing her mind as she pictured Steven's surprise upon receiving the homemade gifts.

Her needles clicked softly in the silence of the room, the only sounds the occasional pop and hiss from the fire and the distant murmur of the ranch hands finishing their day.

She imagined the cozy cabin they would build for Cynthia and Nathaniel. She loved the idea of having friends so close. Yes, they were employees, but they were also friends, and they mattered to her.

Elaina's fingers pressed into the dough, firm and sure, as she rolled it flat on the kitchen table. A dusting of flour coated the surface like the first snowfall, and the scent of molasses and spices hung thick in the air. Beside her, Cynthia lifted cookie cutters—a star, a tree, a bell—and pressed them into the gingerbread with a rhythm as steady as a heartbeat.

"Perfect," Elaina murmured, eyeing the shapes they'd created. Her hands worked almost mechanically, comforted by the task's simplicity. It had been hours since she'd seen Steven, his presence in the house dwindling with each passing day as he retreated to the barn, absorbed in tasks he didn't share.

"Has he mentioned anything to you?" Elaina asked, her voice betraying a hint of concern as she glanced toward the window where the barn stood.

"Steven? Not a word," Cynthia replied, her tone light, though her eyes flicked up to meet Elaina's with an understanding that spoke volumes.

"Perhaps he's just busy," Cynthia offered, but the words did little to ease the knot in Elaina's stomach.

"Perhaps," Elaina echoed, but the uncertainty lingered like a stubborn chill. She wanted to believe it was nothing more than the pressures of the ranch. And yet, part of her feared it was something more personal, a rift growing between them.

The oven door creaked as Elaina opened it and slid the tray of cookies inside, the gingerbread destined to become the walls and roof of a surprise she hoped would make Steven feel like he was home for the holidays.

As they worked, Cynthia chattered about the upcoming Christmas festivities, her cheerfulness a balm to the worry that gnawed at Elaina's mind. They talked of Nathaniel and his new role as foreman, the pride in Cynthia's voice unmistakable when she spoke his name.

"Imagine, if we had our own cabin," Cynthia said, her eyes aglow with the dream of it. Elaina smiled, sharing in her friend's joy, even as her own heart ached for the closeness of a true love match.

"Your cabin will be the heart of the ranch," Elaina assured her. "But you need to marry first." She winked at her friend, who laughed.

Elaina's boots crunched against the freshly fallen snow as she strode purposefully across the yard to where Steven and Beau were conferring beside a towering fir. The sky above was a crisp cerulean, a stark contrast to the white blanket that draped over the landscape. With her breath frosting in the chilly air, Elaina called out to them, her voice ringing clear.

"Beau, we're planning a small gathering for Christmas Eve. Nathaniel, Cynthia, and the Johnsons will be joining us. Can we count on you as well?"

Beau tipped his hat back and flashed a grin as wide as the horizon. "Wouldn't miss it, ma'am."

"Good," Elaina replied. "And we'll need a tree. One worthy of the celebration."

Without another word, Steven turned to the fir and, with an axe in hand, set about his task.

Meanwhile, Elaina returned to the warmth of the kitchen where Cynthia waited with bowls of popcorn and cranberries. Together, they sat by the table, threading needle after needle through the fluffy white kernels and the glossy red berries. The repetitive motion was soothing, and each completed string brought a sense of progress, of something festive taking shape.

"Imagine how lovely these will look, draped around the tree," Cynthia mused, her blue eyes sparkling like the icicles hanging from the eaves outside.

"I can't wait. My father never wanted a tree in the house," Elaina agreed, though her gaze kept drifting toward the window, watching Steven. Each time she glanced out, her heart tugged a little harder. What was it that took him to the barn so often?

"Are you worried about him?" Cynthia's gentle inquiry pulled Elaina back from her reverie.

"Perhaps," Elaina admitted, her fingers pausing in their work. "He's been...distant lately."

"Men have their own ways," Cynthia said with a knowing smile. "But he'll come around, especially tonight. No one can resist the spirit of Christmas Eve."

Elaina wanted to believe her. She threaded another cranberry onto the string, hoping that each small thing she did to prepare for Christmas would bring them closer together.

Outside, the sound of the axe ceased, and after a moment, the fir fell with a soft whoosh, its descent muffled by the snow.

"Looks like we'll have our tree," Elaina murmured, more to herself than to Cynthia. And perhaps, with the tree and the party, a chance to mend what seemed frayed between her and Steven. She wanted everything to feel *right* again.

"Let's go help him bring it in," Cynthia suggested, setting aside her work and standing up.

"All right," Elaina said, a determined spark igniting within her.

THE FRESHLY CUT FIR tree stood in the corner of the living area, its branches reaching out as if to embrace the warmth of the room. Elaina stepped back, her hands on her hips, and examined their handiwork. The popcorn and cranberry garlands draped over the boughs like a festive shawl, while the soft glow from the fireplace danced across the handmade ornaments that adorned the greenery.

"Looks like it's missing something," Cynthia remarked, her gaze following Elaina's.

"Maybe one more string of just the cranberries?" Elaina suggested.

"Perfect." Cynthia clasped her hands together, clearly pleased.

Elaina could not help but share her sentiment. With the tree now almost ready, she felt a surge of hopefulness for the evening ahead. As soon as the last of the cranberries were strung and on the tree, they would be able to move on to the next task at hand.

"Time for the gingerbread house," Elaina announced a short while later, rolling up her sleeves. They had baked the pieces earlier in the week, and now it was time to assemble the confectionery abode.

Working side by side, they pieced together the walls, the roof, and the delicate chimney. Elaina carefully piped icing along the edges, while Cynthia added candy windows and gumdrop decorations. The sweet aroma of ginger and molasses filled the air, mingling with the scent of pine needles.

"Look at it, Elaina," Cynthia beamed, stepping back to admire their creation. "It's like a dream."

"Let's place it where everyone can see it," Elaina suggested, and together they positioned the gingerbread house on the main table, its sugary facade catching the firelight.

As the guests began to arrive, the ranch house buzzed with laughter and conversation. Beau and the Johnsons brought an air of cheer, shaking off the chill from outside with wide smiles and hearty greetings.

Steven put a disc on the gramophone, and it didn't take long before pairs were spinning around the room, caught up in the rhythm and the joy of the season.

Elaina watched as Cynthia and Nathaniel found each other amidst the dancers. There was an ease between them, a silent language spoken through glances and smiles. As the song reached its crescendo,

Nathaniel pulled Cynthia close, whispering something that made her eyes widen with surprise and delight.

The music faded into applause, and Nathaniel's voice carried across the room, steady and sure. "Cynthia, will you marry me?"

Silence hung for a heartbeat before Cynthia's answer rang out clear as a bell. "Yes!" The word tumbled from her lips, wrapped in laughter, and the room erupted in cheers.

Elaina clapped her hands, her heart swelling with happiness for her friend. In this moment, surrounded by the warmth of the gathering and the promise of new beginnings, she could almost believe that everything would turn out just fine.

"Look at them," Steven said, coming to stand beside her. His hand brushed hers, sending a familiar thrill through her.

"Everything's changing," Elaina whispered.

"Change can be good," Steven replied, his gaze holding hers. "It can bring us closer to where we want to be."

Amidst the laughter and merriment, Elaina caught a glimpse of Steven's hand sneaking toward the gingerbread house. With a swift motion, he broke off a shingle from the roof and popped it into his mouth, his hazel eyes twinkling with mischief.

"Steven Miller!" Elaina admonished her tone light and teasing. "You'll have our gingerbread home in ruins before the night's end!"

The room erupted in good-natured laughter as others took notice. Beau, with his hearty chuckle, leaned over to Steven and playfully swatted his shoulder. "Leave some for the rest of us, friend," he joked, while Cynthia shook her head, her eyes dancing with amusement.

"Can't help myself," Steven confessed, grinning sheepishly. "It's just too tempting." He locked eyes with Elaina, and for a moment, their shared smile held a private warmth that only they could understand.

Finally, the clock chimed late into the night, signaling the time for farewells. Yawning guests stretched, their faces aglow with contentment. Steven stood by the door, shaking hands and clapping backs as the Johnsons donned their coats and hats.

"I've got to take care of something," Steven said, his voice carrying a note of urgency that surprised Elaina. She watched him leave with the others, a shadow of confusion crossing her face.

"Goodnight, Elaina," Beau called out. "And Merry Christmas."

"Goodnight," she replied, her voice softer than she intended.

Once the door closed behind the last guest, the house fell silent, save for the whisper of wind outside. Elaina stood alone amidst the remnants of the celebration, the gingerbread house now missing several pieces, a testament to Steven's playful thievery.

When it became obvious Steven wasn't coming right back, Elaina went to bed without him. And as sleep finally claimed her, she clung to the hope that whatever Steven was taking care of, it would lead him back to her, to their newly shared life that seemed to hold so much promise.

Chapter Ten

E laina Miller rubbed sleep from her eyes and gathered her wavy strawberry blonde hair into a loose bun at the nape of her neck. Despite the festive day that lay ahead, she was feeling blue. Steven had come to bed so late last night, she'd not even noticed his arrival.

Pulling her shawl tighter around her shoulders, Elaina moved with purpose, measuring out flour and cracking eggs into a bowl. The silence of the house hung heavy around her, broken only by the occasional pop and hiss from the stovetop. She whisked the batter, each stroke a release for the worry that knitted her brow. Why would Steven prefer to be in the chill of the barn and not in bed with her? It made no sense.

As Elaina poured the batter onto the hot frying pan, the back door creaked open, and Steven Miller stepped inside, his breath misting in the cold air. He stamped the snow from his boots, his broad shoulders silhouetted against the early dawn. In his arms, he cradled a handmade cradle, adorned with a bright red bow that stood out starkly against the rich, dark wood.

"Morning, Elaina," Steven said, his voice a comforting rumble in the quiet of the kitchen.

"Good morning," she replied, tucking a loose strand of hair behind her ear. "You're up early."

"Couldn't let the cows start Christmas without a good milking." His hazel eyes held a spark of something secret, something hopeful.

He set the cradle down near the hearth with care, and from within it, he retrieved a smaller package, wrapped in brown paper and tied with twine. The parcel seemed almost inconsequential nestled within the grandeur of the cradle, yet his gentle handling suggested a treasure beyond measure.

Elaina's gaze lingered on the cradle, tracing the smooth lines of the craftsmanship with an appreciative eye. It was clear that this was what had kept him from their bed until the small hours. The realization that he had been creating something so beautiful made her wonder if she'd misjudged him.

"Steven, the cradle..." Her voice trailed off as she took in the full sight of the gift that would soon rock the baby she carried within her.

"Wait till you see what's inside," Steven said, a boyish grin breaking across his face as he gestured toward the wrapped package.

The scent of pancakes began to fill the room, a homely reminder of the simple pleasures they shared. As Elaina turned the pancakes, her movements became less mechanical. She felt as if the holiday might just turn out to be something special. This Christmas might yet hold more than she had dared to hope for.

Elaina slid the last of the golden-brown pancakes onto a plate, the aroma of sizzling bacon mingling with the sweet scent of the maple syrup she had warmed over the stove. She set the table with a practiced hand, arranging utensils and pouring fresh milk into two glasses.

"Breakfast is ready," she called out.

Steven entered and took his seat at the table. "Smells wonderful," he said, a tender smile touching the corners of his mouth as he reached for her hand to say grace.

They bowed their heads, Elaina feeling the rough texture of his palm, worn from days of laboring on the ranch. She was growing more and more excited at the idea of what was in the cradle. And she couldn't wait for him to see what she'd labored over for him.

"Thank you, Elaina," Steven said, breaking into her thoughts. "This is a fine Christmas breakfast."

"I'm glad you think so. It's a good thing I've learned to cook since Cynthia is getting married. I'm sure she'll still help me, but it won't be quite the same." Her gaze met his. "She's spending the day in town with her folks and Nathaniel."

After breakfast, Elaina gathered the dishes and began to wash them.

She rinsed the last plate and wiped it dry, her movements slow and deliberate. As she wiped her hands on a towel, she caught a glimpse of the cradle once more. He'd carved the design of an angel into the headboard. It was as if he'd created an angel to watch over their baby.

Elaina stepped into the main room, the warmth of the hearth battling the chill that seeped through the walls. Her gaze fell upon the cradle nestled near the fire. It was crafted with care, the wood polished to a honeyed glow that spoke of hours spent sanding and finishing it to perfection. She walked over, her fingers tracing the smooth, curved edges.

"Steven, this is beautiful," she murmured, unable to mask the admiration in her voice. "You made this?" She was almost certain he had.

Steven nodded. "Thank you. I did," Steven replied. "I wanted to finish it before Christmas. That's what kept me in the barn so late last night. I hated leaving you, but I had to get it finished."

Elaina nodded, her lips curving upward in a tentative smile, understanding dawning on her. His late nights were not an escape from their life together but a dedication to their future.

"Here," she said, her tone lightening as she drew closer to where he stood. From beneath the tree, she retrieved a pair of carefully wrapped packages. "I made these for you." The gifts were modest but she'd worked hard on them, and they would help keep him warm throughout the long Montana winter.

Steven's expression softened as he accepted them, his large hands turning them over with reverence. Then, with a gentle smile, he reached into the cradle and brought out a smaller package, extending it to her.

"Your other gift," he said simply, placing it in her outstretched hands.

"Go ahead, open yours first," Elaina urged, her heart pounding with a mix of nerves and excitement. She watched as Steven carefully untied the twine around his presents.

Steven unfolded the knitted scarf, its deep red yarn complementing the golden hue of his hair. "This is mighty fine work, Elaina," he said, wrapping it around his neck and grinning at the way it shielded him from the room's chill. Then he opened the socks and the gloves, pulling the gloves on. "Thank you. I'll treasure these."

With his gifts received and appreciated, Elaina's hands trembled slightly as she turned to the small package he had given her. As she peeled back the layers, she uncovered a wooden ornament, exquisitely carved and polished to a soft sheen.

It was a woman with wavy hair cascading around her shoulders, an infant cradled in her arms. Elaina gasped, her fingers tracing the figure's face, so like her own. The detail was astonishing—from the gentle curve of the cheek to the familiar set of the jaw. A wave of wonder washed over her; Steven had captured not just her likeness but something of her essence, too.

"How—" Her voice caught, and she cleared her throat. "How did you manage to make this?"

"Every spare moment I had," he confessed, standing closer now. "I wanted to give you something that spoke of us, of hope."

Elaina looked up at him, her eyes wide with amazement. The ornament was the most beautiful gift she'd ever received. She could not believe that he—the quiet man who had come into her life as a stranger—had taken such care to create something so personal, so touching.

"Steven, it's..." Words failed her as she struggled to express the depth of her appreciation. She simply held the ornament out between them, letting the silent eloquence of the carving convey what she could not.

Tears brimmed in Elaina's eyes as she clutched the delicate wooden figure to her chest.

"Steven, this..." Her voice trembled like the flicker of candlelight against a dark winter's morn. "It's perfect. I love it so much."

"I thought I could make a new ornament for you every year, and we could fill the Christmas tree with them. Since you never had a tree, I know you didn't have any to begin with."

The room seemed to hold its breath, the warmth from the stove embracing them as the scent of pine from the Christmas tree lingered in the air. Steven stepped forward, his presence solid and reassuring. He reached out, his rough fingers gently wiping away a tear that traced a path down her rosy cheek.

"Elaina," he said, his voice deep and resonant, "I needed to make something as perfect as you are." His hand rested lightly on her shoulder, the weight of his touch anchoring her amidst the swell of emotions. "I love you."

She clasped the wooden ornament to her breast, its edges pressing into the fabric of her dress as if it sought to become part of her. Her lips parted, a breath of air escaping as she searched for words that might mirror the depth of her feelings.

"Steven," she whispered. "I love you."

A silence fell between them, heavy with the gravity of their confessions. Elaina watched as Steven's Adam's apple bobbed—a mute testament to his own tumultuous emotions—and she saw the subtle shift of muscle beneath the fabric of his shirt as he moved closer to her.

"Elaina," he said again. "We've already been through a lot together, you and I."

"Yes," she agreed, her voice steadier now. "And now I know that even if I lost the ranch, I'd get through it as long as you were beside me."

"Elaina," Steven began again. "I reckon we're in this for the long haul."

"I know I am. I never dreamed when I wrote that letter to your sister that I'd end up with a man who was not only a partner in business, but the man I wanted to spend the rest of my life with. I'm so thankful you were the one who responded to me and not someone else."

"I cannot imagine a future without you in it. I know we skipped the courtship part of our relationship, but I hope you'll feel like I'm courting you every day for the rest of our lives." Steven leaned down and kissed Elaina softly. "You are exactly what I needed in my life."

Epilogue

Ten years later, Elaina looked down at the babies suckling at each of her breasts. The girls were perfect and identical to one another. Jed, her firstborn, was out helping his father on the ranch, and Cynthia sat beside her in a rocker. "Do you need anything?"

Elaina shook her head. "How could I? I have a husband who dotes on me, a friend who helps me with all the chores, and six children who make me crazy with their antics. Well, I assume these two will in a year or two." The infants were only a month old, and they hadn't yet learned to pester their siblings and make them yell.

Cynthia smiled. "My two boys are out there with Jed. Your three younger boys are up in the treehouse, where you told them not to go."

Elaina sighed. "Their father can deal with them. If only he'd built a ladder to go up into the house like I asked and not those easy steps they can all climb..."

Cynthia laughed. "They just get to play in it longer this way!"

"That's true." She looked down at little Hope and Grace. "At least I got two girls finally. I thought I'd end up with a dozen boys and no girls. Of course, Steven says we need another couple dozen children."

"I'm glad I'm too old for more," Cynthia said.

"I have a good seven or eight years of childbearing left. I guess I could lock Steven from my bedroom..."

The door of the house burst open. "I heard that!" Steven said from the doorway. "You need to watch what you say when the windows are open!"

Elaina laughed. "You need to watch what you listen to!" She knew Steven wouldn't believe she would ever do such a thing, and the look of mock-anger on his face made her laugh all the harder.

Steven walked to her, his eyes on the babies in her arms. "Thanks for giving me two beautiful girls to spoil."

"And to bake you gingerbread houses?"

"That too." He dropped a kiss on her forehead. "I'll be back in a bit. Jed and I are going to town to get more nails. Repairing fences is a never-ending project around here."

"You wanted the life of a rancher."

"And I love every minute of it." He raised his hand in a wave as he headed out the door, wrapping an arm around the shoulders of their son, Jed. "Someday, you're going to be as blessed as I am, son."

Elaina didn't hear anything else Steven said to their son, but she looked down at her daughters, hoping one day they would be as blessed as she was. Love surrounded them.

www.ingramcontent.com/pod-product-compliance
Lightning Source LLC
Chambersburg PA
CBHW031437130726
47989CB00003B/1178